GRIN'S

FAIRY TALES

DARKWATER

First published in 2025 by Darkwater Books
An imprint of Harris Oxford Limited.
6-7 Citibase, New Barclay House, 234 Botley Road,
Oxford, England, OX2 0HP

ISBN 978-1-909072-47-3

This book

is dedicated to beautiful readers with excellent taste.

I am..... a writer

GRIN'S

FAIRY TALES

SUNDAY PATTISON

ILLUSTRATED BY

JIM ANDERSON

DARKWATER

My Miraculous Birth

I am Grin, the perpetual grin.

Before anything else there is me.

On the day I hit the planet, blizzards scrubbed the land clean of people and warmth, snow hammered the houses like bullets, and the sky turned such a dazzling white that each snowflake seemed black. I was born early in the morning, and a comet was discovered by a Hawaiian observatory at the very instant that I gave my first, mighty howl of triumph.

Precocious from the start, I blasted out of the womb sporting a full head of curly black hair. When placed with the other new arrivals, I was already able to move about — and that energy which always coils within me, made me twist and turn in my hospital crib.

Once my father finished puffing his seven, celebratory *Wetschina* cigars, he came to pay his respects (he did not feel the need to witness my birth, having witnessed the conception). Father, encountered a neat row of babies, all lined up in their cribs... except one.

I lay crosswise, flexing my muscles and desperate to meet my public. I was alive and had things to do.

My proud mother and I, were soon out of hospital. We went straight back to our Austrian Alps. Even then, I had a strong idea of where I wanted to be, and flat, oppressive lands did not appeal. I was created to leapfrog boulders, and race through wild forests, not to play computer games in overdeveloped, human sheep-pen towns.

So, I grew up in the Alps, where the canyons surrounding us are the canyons of our minds. Each person is their own myth, remaking the landscape and mythology that made them.

We are fairy tales.

Before I could walk, I would gatevault out of my cot, crawling into cupboards, which I often overturned. Every item of furniture had to be weighted, or nailed down (locking me in my bedroom proved pointless, because I quickly learnt to pick the lock). I was given the honorific title of *Bims,* because I was always bimsing everything and everybody. Practicing swallow dives out of my high chair, I knew I was destined for greatness.

I learnt to read way before my comrades in Kindergarten, overdosing on books of heroic myths, because I have ever been heroically mythological. Teachers, complained that I was not following the expected, slow and shallow trajectory of learning, whereby, boys agree to condemn themselves as the unbookish cause of all humanity's misfortunes.

By the time I was six, I was excused reading classes, because my parents saw:

teachers are simply impediments to my greatness.

I could finally read those stories my teachers disapproved of, without their censorious, virtue-signalling nonsense. I rewrote myths to include myself. I became the kind of boy who skips three steps at once, and shoots old men's hats off with a homemade bow and arrow.

The Austrian Alps are a Pagan country. There are festivals to drive out darkness. There are festivals to make crops and babies grow. There are graveyards in forests, so friendly trees can absorb souls and exhale them into Heaven. Christian priests here, are pragmatists who have never dragged people away from invigorating superstitions.

I am balanced on a knife-edge of savagery and civilisation, combining roaring glee with exquisite sophistication. From an early age, there was only one possible vocation for me: writing.

Writing is glamorous.

Every popstar, actor, comedian, athlete, fashion designer, model, photographer, film director, celebrity, influencer — and whore — just longs to be an author. The first thing they do, once they are famous and have exhausted their own little talent, is squeeze out a book.

I am more farsighted than that: I have missed out any pretence of a career, and gone straight for the literary jugular.

My name is, Grin. I am a wordaholic.

I spark readers into empathy — you have to invent the thoughts, sounds, and images I describe. This separates me from artists in other disciplines, who do not make their audiences work.

A moviemaker is a dictator, beaming visions into passive recipients. A painter, like a photographer, imposes their eyes on the viewer. A sculptor is a photographer who uses braille. A composer is a hypnotist. But I am... a writer.

I provide myths now wonder has been tortured to death by the Internet.

I force minds out of skulls and into skulls. I make my audiences live different lives. I train imaginations, to sympathise with their story-telling ancestors, and with every single individual who makes up a crowd.

I am large and handsome and brave.

And, I make things up.

On the day I was born, blizzards scrubbed the land clean of people and warmth. Snow hammered the houses like bullets, and the sky turned such a dazzling white that each snowflake seemed black. I was born early in the morning, and a comet was discovered by a Hawaiian observatory at the very instant I gave my first, mighty howl of triumph.

Writers must roar — or, shut up forever.

BEATING THE DEVIL

Four years had passed since my grand entrance. I was staying at my grandparents' house. I looked out of the window of the upstairs kitchen I slept in. The sky was ashen. The clock ticked like a dripping tap. The mountains hid their faces in their clouds, fed up with looking at me.

I had bet myself that if I leapt the six floorboards to my bed, I would live to be a hundred.

I missed.

So, I bet myself that I would leap them on a second attempt... or, the Devil would reach out from under the bed (where he lived) and grab my soul.

I missed.

I would roast in Hell, while imps prodded me with big forks to see if I was done through.

Desperation sped my thoughts. I needed God to help me. Perhaps, if I knocked on Heaven, *He* would answer the door? Clouds waved at me from the mountains like the Devil's own, cheeky handkerchiefs.

The mountains were taunting me.

What if, I jumped out of the window and jabbed the descending clouds, to prove my faith in God? I looked down from my window.

The ground seemed to suck me in, until the tips of my fingers tingled and I became dizzy. The lawn, shone, temptingly green and darkly fluorescent in the grey light.

I was scared, but I had to jump — my soul was at stake.

One — two — THREE!

I could not do it.

I heard imps whistling as they stoked their fires for me, and sharpened the prongs of great forks. I was too frightened of heights, as well as of Hell. I had to overcome a great fear to deal with my greater fear.

One — two — THREE!

I flung myself at Heaven.

I crashed in the roses.

I rose again, pricked by thorns. I needed to sneak back into the house. The door was locked just as firmly against the resurrected, as it was against the rampaging pillagers of my grandparents' nightmares.

So, I rang the doorbell. My tombstone-blond, grizzled grandfather, answered, surprised — then, annoyed — to see me outdoors.

Neither grandparent, believed, or wanted to believe, that I hopped out of an upstairs window. My grandfather spotted a crack in a drainpipe, *proving* I had shinned down.

I was sent to bed early for trying to scare my grandparents. I bounced up and down on it for an hour, to punish the Devil underneath.

KRAMPUS

Every saint has an embarrassing friend.

In the Alps, St. Nicholas' hirsute embarrassment is called *Krampus*, has long black fur and horns, and a tongue lolling down to his navel. He drags chains, and carries birch twigs for thrashing naughty people.

Oh, and he has huge metal clappers attached to his buttocks.

Krampus is a party animal. Nobody really knows how he got here. Perhaps, he met St. Nicholas when they were drunk, at some Heaven and Hell *cheese-and-wine party*? Perhaps, they now cohabit like two sweet old queens, indulging their need to dress up and party just once a year, on December the sixth... though Krampus also goes out by himself a day earlier.

St. Nicholas does not mind Krampus going out to party by himself. St. Nicholas is a saint and never gets jealous.

Anyway, on December the sixth, when St. Nicholas brings, chocolate, oranges, and nuts, for good children — who leave their boots outside their doors to be filled with his gifts — bad children, by some oversight, also receive, chocolate, oranges, and nuts.

Krampus no longer really punishes the naughty... which is a good thing for me. Krampus, has retired, and become an excuse for youths to wear scary masks and playfully hit friends on their rumps. The friend usually runs away giggling, knowing full well that Krampus is Seppl, who lives down the road and has a crush on her. Sometimes, the girl even dresses up as Krampus, and comes back to hit Seppl on the rump.

Every child knows Krampus is a bluff — unlike St. Nicholas, in his flamboyant purple robes with white fur trim, whose huge beard covers an affectionate heart. Krampus, exists to be hissed at by children, and smiled at by people with springy buttocks. Even as a five-year-old, I understood this.

So, I perched in the wood-lined living room, snug with my mother, excitedly awaiting the arrival of those two confirmed bachelors — St. Nicholas and his uncouth friend — when there was a rattle of chains outside the window, and a bone-chilling laugh: a laugh that pierced me to my marrow, from someone Hell held no fears for. I knew such a laugh could only come from my grandfather.

Ever heroic and courageous (as my destiny intended) I yelled — "Zwetschgen Krampus!" — and dived under the table. The chains rattled like a skeleton on a gibbet. Krampus tapped on the window with his horns. Fierce laughter reverberated around the living room.

I again yelled — "Zwetschgen Krampus!" — and realised that hardly anyone reading this, knows what a *Zwetschgen Krampus* is.

A Zwetschgen Krampus is a Krampus made from prunes — a traditional present on December the fifth. I was implying that my grandfather was wrinkled and edible, which seemed incredibly funny to me when I was five and still seems funny now he is dead.

It also amused my mother, who clapped her hands, and my grandfather — who came in, cold and dishevelled, pretending that he did not know what the commotion was.

When I was slightly older and wickeder, I wanted to be Krampus myself. I wore a paper Krampus mask and hid behind trees, waiting for unwary older girls — so I could leap out and slap their bottoms, the curviness of which fascinated me.

Specifically, there was Bärbl, who had achieved the unimaginable age of twenty-two. She was the archetype of hourglasses... a jiggly, bosomy, buttocky girl, whose pendulous seat demanded to be slapped.

I knew that she took flowers to her family grave in the forest cemetery, so I hid behind a snowy fir as dusk glowed on the mountains, hoping she would appear.

The air was still. Candles, burnt and flickered in red jars on graves, commemorating the loved ones beneath them.

And, then... I saw Bärbl approaching: a panoply of rolling curves, a fleshly temptation, a *goddess* needing to be conquered. Her blonde curls were hidden by a woolly hat, her nose was red, but her lips — O, even her lips were curvy! She wore lycra skiing trousers, which accentuated her body, and a thick jumper — which did the same. It was impossible for Bärbl to hide her glory.

I waited until she passed me, then, stealthily — treacherously like a golden jackal — crept up behind her.

My hand coiled back — it had to be united with the rotating globes of her posterior — and struck home.

Bärbl, screamed, and flowers showered down, as she turned to face me. Cawing crows scattered in the trees.

Bärbl grabbed me.

I bit her finger and ran.

Bärbl, pursued me, more like an express train than a conquered goddess. Suddenly, I was Krampus no more, but a little boy sprinting through the snow.

The distance between my footprints and Bärbl's, grew smaller and smaller, until there was a violent disturbance of snow... with me in it.

Bärbl tore off my mask, and ground snow into my face until my skin was as red and sore as the sunset.

I know why Krampus retired.

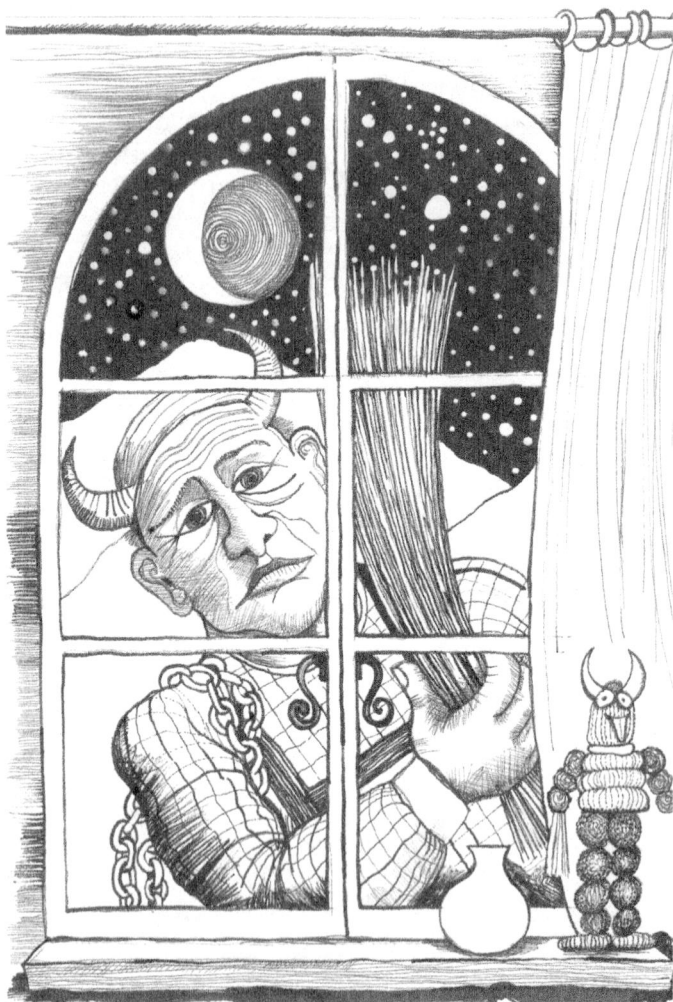

OMA

Never trust your grandmother, especially if she is Austrian.

This is not to say Austrian grandmothers are more dishonest, or dangerous, than other grannies — but they do have a talent for adjusting the truth. Austrian grandmothers are artists, and remake reality to protect the innocence of children.

My grandmother, known as *Oma*, was a fit, attractive woman with a smile ever to hand, who cycled up and down Alps. Oma had brown eyes and dark hair, and an unlined face. She sang, apparently guilelessly, in a sinless church choir. But, like all grandmothers, there is more to her than that.

Oma's ability to retune reality, showed itself in how she managed my relationship with my great-grandmother, *Ur-Oma*.

Ur-Oma had reached the end of her life, and, not having died yet, spent her days in a continual re-run of the past. Her small bedroom became the marble hunting lodge she knew as a young woman in the southern Tirol. I became the horseman who courted her.

Lucky for me, her courtship had been polite.

Mostly.

There was one time when Ur-Oma told me: her parents were out and their double-bed was free for us to use.

This puzzled me.

Oma, explained that Ur-Oma was telling me: Ur-Oma's parents had gone to Heaven, and no longer needed their bed. So, I could have the bed when I was old enough.

I am still waiting.

Then, Ur-Oma left our world altogether, and lost any idea of day and night, and forgot how to speak. She lay in bed, night and day, sighing and bleating.

"What's that?" — I would ask Oma, who assured me, it was a stray goat, which had wandered into the village from Klackl's field.

On nights Ur-Oma was especially loud, Oma swore dreadful (yet decorous) oaths that she would deal with Farmer Klackl, and his incompetently erected fences, at the very first glimmer of day.

I began to resent goats and how they disrupted my sleep, but, more than that — I resented Ur-Oma for impersonating goats at four in the morning.

Ur-Oma died.

One morning, I woke to find Oma, bustling around like an ant in the Sun. And *no,* Oma said, I could not go into Ur-Oma's room to see the body. Everything that Ur-Oma had touched, was infected with corpse poison *(Leichengift),* and needed to be disinfected.

Oma's reworkings of the truth were inspired by folklore, and became part of the landscape of my brain. She was the person who first told me about the *Wild Hunt,* spirits that gallop across the sky on nights when fierce lightning crackles.

I learnt that milk went off because the Stormbride, who trails the hunt, turns it sour to show she has noticed you. Oma also told me of her brother, my great-uncle Martin, the famed poet and cigarette smoke-ring exhaler, who, when even smaller than I was then, boldly asked the valet of Emperor Franz Josef to do his Lederhosen's button flies up for him.

The Emperor, a great and good man, who personally attended to the welfare of every last one of his subjects, graciously granted permission for my great-uncle Martin to have his flies done up.

Oma gave me a book, titled *Verschlungen,* of tales collected from old people in the locality.

"Read this." — she said, tapping the cover — "The canyons of your mind, transform every stream that flows through them. One day, you will write down the stories in *Verschlungen* — and they will have changed because you read them, to become one of the best books ever written."

I did not then understand what she was talking about. But, I remembered what she said until I was old enough to understand. Oma gave the book to me because she knew my childhood in Austria was ending.

Every New Year's Eve, Oma told our fortunes for the coming year — by melting lead over the stove, and dripping it into a pan of cold water from a spoon. The lead, set in weird, asteroidal lumps, which only Oma could interpret.

Eager to learn Oma's secret, I examined these lumps over and over again, and attempted to extract meaning from them. I saw nothing. Oma had a gift for prophesy I did not inherit.

One New Year's Eve, she looked at the frozen splash of lead that mapped out my year ahead, and told me: I would fly faraway, to England. And, sure enough, a month later, I was in flat, chilly England, the stories of *Verschlungen* flowing through my mind, keeping me warm — changing, as I change.

THE WILDENSTEIN LADY

It was the last gasp of Summer — a hot, overcast day, threatened the mountains with thunder. The birds and crickets were mute, bored with the songs they had performed so long for an unappreciative public. The green forest sagged with moisture and heat.

Something had to happen... so, a raindrop fell, and stung the face of the thin, blue-eyed, bleach-blond, backpacker panting up the mountain-side. He was as oblivious to this warning shot, as anyone wearing a NO-KANGAROOS-IN-AUSTRIA tee-shirt could be.

Jimi — the backpacker — was a modish guy, who had globally puffed his way through veritable breeze-blocks of dope. Jimi enjoyed bungee-jumping, skateboarding, and experimenting with chemical euphorias. He regarded other cultures as carveries for the vegan meat of his traveller's tales: that special wisdom of exotic people, who kindly live in misery to aid tourists' quests for personal growth.

Now, Jimi was struggling up a mountain slope in Austria, and slowly discovering, step by arduous step, that Eco-tourism sucked. The people were European (hence, unexotic) and the drugs were fairtrade (hence, expensive). There were too many trees. And, you were expected to walk. But.. Jimi's parents (who paid for their son's trip) thought, rambling in the Alps was just the thing to straighten Jimi out.

Rambling was an unusual activity for Jimi, because it did not involve Jimi paying somebody for a thrill that demanded no effort on Jimi's part. It is true, Jimi was a skateboard enthusiast, and this did involve more effort than Jimi's other hobby of dropping off a platform on the end of a bungee rope — but, mostly, *skating* involved Jimi cluttering up backpacker bars with his sidewalk surfer while rolling a joint.

Today, Jimi was searching for the ruins of Castle Wildenstein, and an imminent storm was on his back — and no matter who, or what, Jimi might throw money at, he was not going to get there any faster. As a lonely raindrop splashed onto his face, Jimi reflected on the tale of derring-do he would tell back home: of the massive Alpine thunderstorm he braved to explore a castle named like a heavy metal band.

WILDENSTEIN... the name had to mean *Wild-Rock*, not *Wild-One-Litre-Measure-Of-Beer,* as Jimi initially surmised.

When Jimi found Wildenstein, he was disappointed. Wildenstein's ruins were not impressive, nothing like Stonehenge, or Angkor Wat — nor even, like the toy plastic castle, Jimi had snapped together as a little boy. Wildenstein was not the most romantic place Jimi had visited.

Wildenstein was not romantic at all.

And, someone else had climbed up here to be disappointed. Jimi, noticed a shimmery girl standing by a broken wall... she was shimmery because she wore a long, translucent white dress, studded with silver stars. Her skin was pale, her lips were blood-red, and her black tresses touched her hips. Her emerald eyes studied Jimi. She was probably the only beautiful woman ever to have studied Jimi.

"Wicked." — thought, Jimi. The reprimanding raindrop that hit his cheek, made Jimi realise he was blushing.

"Hello, you!"— said, the beautiful girl — "Don't worry, Jimi... I won't bite."

"Wicked!" — thought Jimi, for a second time, and forgot to ask why she knew his name and spoke English. Then again... Jimi had smoked dope with an awful lot of English-speakers worldwide that he could never remember.

"Hi!" — said, Jimi — "What's an ugly girl like you doing in a nice place like this?"

(Jimi always used *humour* to start a conversation with attractive people.)

"It's a long story, Jimi." — said, the girl —"I'll tell it to you anyway. Maybe, you can help me?"

This disturbed Jimi.

Jimi was not keen on damsels in distress, being a gender-fluid feminist himself. But, like all female feminists, the beautiful girl just carried on talking... "I'm not like the other girls you know, Jimi.

Actually, I'm the cursed maiden of Wildenstein, and I'm over nine hundred years old. Not bad for my age, eh?"

She thrust out her bosom.

Jimi suddenly wanted to kiss her, but a large and timely raindrop slapped his face. And the beautiful feminist just carried on talking...

"Where you see ruins and undergrowth, I see the castle of my ancestors. Its great towers and walls, overlooked this valley, and its drawbridge mocked all our enemies' ambitions. Our men-at-arms, guarded the road below for travelling merchants. Unfortunately, watching rich merchants pass by, day after day after day, grew too much for my ancestors, so they started robbing the merchants they were supposed to protect from robbers, kidnapping them for ransom, even, torturing them in our dungeons for fun.

"There was a lot less to entertain us in those days, you see: no Internet, no nightclubs, no skateboards — nothing, except drinking, eating, fighting, and bonking. Oh, and the odd church service."

(NO SKATEBOARDS! — Jimi could totally understand why the cursed maiden's ancestors had turned to banditry.)

And the beautiful feminist carried on talking... "My father, tried to curb his own tendency to have naughty fun. He stopped robbing and torturing passers-by. He even rode escort for the merchants' baggage trains. But one day, a different kind of traveller visited us — a bejewelled Crusader freshly returned from the Holy Land, dressed in silk, sporting a beard cut in the Arab manner.

"Usually, Crusades are a very good way of using up religious lunatics — you just get them to attack religious lunatics of another faith, they martyr each other, and both lots of lunatic go to Heaven. Yet, this Crusader had not only survived, but thrived.

"During the feast to welcome the Crusader to Wildenstein, Daddy decided that he'd rather be a robber baron — rather be a chamber pot scrubber! — than listen to some pious know-it-all witter on about chopping up Saracens. And it was fashionable at the time, to kidnap Crusaders. No castle could call itself contemporary or complete, if it didn't have at least one Crusader languishing in its dungeons. My father was only going to kidnap and rob the Crusader, and maybe torture him a little bit. He didn't really want to lock him up forever.

"But... the Crusader would keep on praying: every drink, every course — every burp — was another excuse to pray. My father (normally, a pious man) became more and more impatient, not wishing to interrupt any prayer with violence. In the end, my father couldn't stand it any longer. Can you blame Daddy for forgetting his good manners? He had the Crusader seized and chained up.

"*Pray your way out of that!* — yelled my father, as he slammed the dungeon door and made off with our guest's jewellery. Unfortunately, the Crusader did exactly as my father told him.

"The Crusader seemed to have developed some sort of special relationship with God while abroad. I well remember his shouted words... *Cower, you thieving knave! Tonight, I will put an end to your miserable family, and to this nest of thieving ravens. I spit on your chains and I vomit you all to Hell.* Then, the Crusader shrugged off his chains, and the dungeon's door burst open.

"Daddy was surprised (as you can imagine) but he wasn't going to let some religious gobshite spoil the evening. Enough was enough. The Crusader was still shouting... *Cursed for all eternity are you and those of your blood. Heaven, will destroy you, and this wretched castle, with a thunderstorm!*

"So, Daddy chopped the Crusader's head off. "The torches throughout the castle flickered, the mastiffs howled, and the ground began to tremble. Rain pelted down. A pitchfork of lightning stabbed Wildenstein, and the castle exploded into lumps of burning rubble, which buried my father, his followers — and ME — for ever.

"Since that day, I've been doomed to wander these ruins, waiting for some brave

young man to break the curse put on me.
Not really a fair punishment, given that I
didn't do anything. I can't help feeling
God's a bit thoughtless some times.

"Anyway, Jimi, I'm telling you this
because you're the brave young man, fated
by the astrological chart of your birth to
rescue me from the Crusader's curse. If you
succeed, you get to marry me!"

"Hey, this feminist really can talk!" —
thought, Jimi. Jimi only agreed to help her
because he was bored with standing under
a hot, dark sky, waiting for a thunderstorm
to happen, listening to some Mediaeval
leftover prattling on about long ago. He did
not want to get wet, or be stabbed by
lightning. He did not fancy marriage much
either — but, the beautiful old girl just
carried on talking... "I knew that you'd help
me, Jimi! How could you turn down the
chance to win all this?"

She thrust out her bosom again.

"It won't be easy, Jimi. You have to find
a blessed palm leaf, and gather quite a lot
of fern. Then come up here for midnight
tonight, and lay a circle of fern on the
ground, to protect yourself against evil
spirits, curses, and any other nasty stuff
that might be floating about.

"I'll appear to you at nought o'clock
precisely — not in the sexy form that you
see before you now, but as a terrible, nine-
headed dragon. (Not my choice of monster,
believe me. I've acquired a new head for

every hundred years that I've been stuck here: God knows why! — or, maybe, He doesn't know at all, and just does these things without thinking.) And I won't be able to help myself, not being myself — and I'll attack you. That's where the palm leaf comes in.

"You have to gently tap each head with the leaf, to make it disappear. If you show the slightest hesitation, or fear, I get another hundred years of hanging around this ruin. And an extra head. But... if you succeed in destroying all my heads as they belch and slaver at you, I'll be saved. You'll be my hero — and I'll be eternally grateful to you, no matter how depraved your sexual desires are."

Jimi had limited knowledge of maidens and their problems, but he guessed this problem was tougher than most. Getting hold of a blessed palm leaf, and finding out what a fern looked like — that was like *botany.*

Botany wasn't Jimi's thing, despite his occasional cultivation of marijuana. Jimi was not so worried about the nine heads: his circle of fern (whatever that was) would surely protect him. And, anyway, how scary could a feminist be if she was sexy and needed to be rescued?

So, Jimi left the beautiful girl still talking to herself, and wandered back to near the town of Bad Ischl, where he was staying in a Bed-and Breakfast called the

Dämmerungshof. He was determined to save the cursed maiden of Wildenstein and bring her back as his bride, to show off to his skater pals.

Renewal was in the air.

The storm had moved on to the next valley without disgorging rain. Sunlight lit up the mountains. The forest sparkled as Jimi descended on Ischl, on the way to his digs.

Jimi was not quite as slow as he seemed to others, so it did not take him long to find a florist that stocked palms. He broke off a long leaf (*"whoops, sorry"*), dipped it in the font at the local church of St. Nicholas, to bless it, and secreted it in his cargo pants. He even looked up ferns online. Once he had studied photos of ferns, he picked some sprigs of the plant in the woods, went back to his bed-and-breakfast, set his alarm clock for 10pm. and took a nap.

The alarm went off on time, but too early.

It was one of those mistimed wake-ups, which leave the wakee feeling groggily clumsy. Jimi did not feel so organised and optimistic, not now that night had quietly beaten the mountains black and blue. But, he trusted his sense of direction, which had never failed him in all his years of dope smoking. Jimi set off into the forest.

The night-time scents of plants and trees, soothed his nervousness as he went. The full Moon illuminated the greenery,

and the cool air made this climb easier
than in the afternoon. He soon reached the
ruins of Castle Wildenstein.

Jimi took the fern from his backpack,
laid it out in a ring, sat down inside the
circle, and waited.

The full Moon was doing its best to
inject romance into the scene, but —
despite the view of the forested mountains,
and the lights from the houses, twinkling
below — the Moon, failed.

Jimi was just a backpacker, sitting
amongst a pile of old rubble, up a
mountain in Austria, waiting for some
weird girl-dragon monster to show up. To
pass the time, Jimi practiced swatting
imaginary dragon heads. He was still
swatting away when the bells of St.
Nicholas struck midnight.

The cursed maiden of Wildenstein
appeared out of the blue air: her body was
naked and heavy and scaly, her hands and
feet were hairy, her nine heads snaked out
of her shoulders on long serpent necks,
and all her contorted faces were terrifying
parodies of femininity.

Jimi realised, just how scary a girl can
be.

One terrible head lashed out at him,
and, as it came close, the head growled:
"Make love to me, make love to me, make
love to me." Jimi clutched the palm leaf
tightly, and tapped the head. The head
vanished, but another was already darting

towards Jimi, and this one howled: "I want a baby, I want a baby, I want a baby." Jimi gathered all his reserves of courage to tap the head, and it vanished. An even more terrible head was already hurtling towards him, and this one barked: "Marry me, marry me, marry me." Jimi was shaking with fear, but years of bungee jumping had steeled his nerves, so this head too, was despatched. Another ugly head was threatening him, and this one rasped: "I need a man, I need a man, I need a man."

This was too much.

Jimi, fainted.

When Jimi woke, the birds were singing. There was dew on the fern and the hot Sun was up.

Jimi's back was stiff, his head was sore — and he had failed. The cursed maiden of Wildenstein would grow yet another head, and be trapped for yet another hundred years — and, ever since, on nights when the Moon is full, and the breeze whispers in the treetops around Wildenstein, you can hear a beautiful girl's voice, softly moaning about the inadequacy of modern men.

THE OLD MAN OF THE ZIMNITZ

If you wander beyond the village of Kreutern — up into the mountain forest — and shadow the stream, you come to the Zimnitz Wilderness. Here, the landscape and greenery of higher regions has spilled over into the valley, and the trees rustle with secrets that rarely, if ever, reveal themselves.

A refugee from Ukraine, called Kalyna, lived in this valley with her daughter, Natalka. Kalyna was an unconvinced widow, who hoped against hope for the return of a husband who lay, dead and lost, in the earth of her homeland. Kalyna lived for her sixteen-year-old daughter, who carried on living only because of her mother's determination they must both stay alive for the father's return.

Kalyna and Natalka, lived by themselves in a dilapidated wooden house scheduled for demolition, which had been redesignated an *asylum hostel*. They earned money by gathering mushrooms, berries, and herbs, which they sold at the weekly organic food market in Bad Ischl.

Despite eating nothing but healthy vegetables, Kalyna sickened from some unknown cause. The local doctor, offered no help beyond prescribing antidepressants — which did no good. Kalyna and her daughter, knew, Kalyna was dying. So, when a posh, stall-holding crone at the organic food market, described a miraculous healing plant that grew only in the Zimnitz, Natalka was determined to try it on her mother.

Natalka started her search for the miracle herb of the Zimnitz on St. John's Day — a day, which invests healing plants with special power. Natalka, searched in the forest — and searched — and searched.. and ignored all the mushrooms and berries that she found, and would usually have rejoiced over. She even left alone the rare berries of the Adlitz tree.

Exhausted, Natalka sat down beneath a small, sheer cliff called the *Trefferwand*. Thin, sparkling rivulets, ran down the rock wall, and the constant, gentle sound of the trickling water, and the soughing of the trees, soon lulled Natalka to sleep.

A bright light gatecrashed Natalka's twitching eyelids, and forced her to look up. She saw a tall, broad man, with long white hair and a shaggy beard that hung down to his belt. He was dressed in a plain, white linen robe, and carried a staff carved from a single tree root.

Natalka fretted that he was a ghost, because he seemed to glow in the shade. He coughed politely, then spoke... "I know what you are searching for, my dear, but you are wasting your time. There is no healing plant to help your mother. Please, follow me."

The old man rapped on the cliff with his staff, and the rock cracked open. Natalka followed the man into the mountain, not really knowing why she was doing so. She wondered if she was dreaming.

A misty light adhered to the interior walls — the same light as adhered to the old man's skin. Thousands of little plants grew in crystal jars that were scattered throughout the cave. ("Is this a drugs factory?" — thought Natalka, remembering some gangsters she knew) Some plants had many leaves — some, had only a few, or none. Some were green, some were wilting, and some had withered. The old man bent down and picked up two jars.

"Look closely, my dear. This is the plant of your mother's life."

The old man thrust one of the jars at Natalka. The plant inside was brown and skeletal, except for half a solitary leaf, on which a fat, yellow worm was munching.

"And this, my dear, is the plant of your life."

The old man withdrew Kalyna's plant and proffered the other jar. The plant inside was healthily green and had sixteen, trefoil leaves, one for each year of Natalka's life so far. The old man, said, "All the people who live here, my dear — and all people, everywhere on Earth — have a hidden seed, which is planted in a jar at their conception, and which grows into a plant that flourishes, and wanes, as their life does. Even if I instantly killed the worm gnawing at your mother's life, it would still be too late for her."

The worm wriggled obscenely.

Natalka knew, the old man was telling the truth. The old man shrugged his shoulders, and explained — "No medicine can cure your mother, because her time is done, my dear. I am sorry, but there is simply no room for everyone to be alive on the same planet at once." Natalka started crying silently, despite herself. But, the old man had seen too many tears over the centuries to be sympathetic. He stared vacantly at Natalka.

"I'm sorry." — said Natalka, embarrassed by her own weakness.

The old man, sighed... "I am sorry too, my dear, but there is nothing I can do. You might help your mother... but, you would have to die in her place."

Natalka nodded, encouraging the old man to continue speaking.

"I could swap the plants between the jars, my dear — your mother would live another few years, but you will die within six months. Do you really want me to do that?"

Wiping away tears, Natalka nodded. She thought of her mother being happily reunited with her father. She wondered, if she would be blessed with a little sister after her own death.

"Very well then." — said the old man. He carefully took the plants out of their jars and swapped them, without spilling any earth. Then, he plucked three leaves from the healthy plant, and gave them to Natalka.

"These are leaves of what was your life's plant, my dear — the plant that some people call, *the miracle herb of the Zimnitz*. But, the herb is always someone else's life. Nobody, can live longer without somebody else living less, or staying unborn.

"Your mother is very close to death, and must eat three years of your young life just to begin to get well. After that, she may enjoy years of good health — sadly, unwitnessed by you."

Natalka awoke in front of the Trefferwand. She lay on the earth, and the Sun was setting behind the mountain peaks. Only three, trefoil leaves in her lap, proved that she had not been dreaming. Natalka got up, and began the long walk back to the house. Her steps seemed more tiring than usual, and her back would not straighten. Natalka shambled home like her sick mother would have done.

At home, Natalka went straight to her mother's bed, and begged her to eat the three leaves of the miracle herb of the Zimnitz — which Kalyna did, despite her own, weary scepticism about ever getting well.

Kalyna fell into a deep, untroubled sleep until the next afternoon, when she awoke, refreshed for the first time in months. As more days passed, Kalyna strengthened and Natalka declined.

Kalyna did not understand, why Fate had played another cruel trick on them, after being so nearly murdered by the little Narcissist in the Kremlin and his horde. She called the doctor — who was as puzzled by Natalka's illness as he had been by Kalyna's — and duly prescribed, antidepressants.

Natalka said nothing.

Desperately, fearfully, Kalyna, exhorted Natalka to stay alive for her father's return. Kalyna, spent half the night on her knees, praying. Natalka's health worsened.

One night, when Kalyna and Natalka had fallen asleep, a bright light disturbed Kalyna's twitching eyelids, and forced her to look up. The old man of the Zimnitz had crept into their bedroom. She had no idea who he was, but remembered the Russians who had forced their way into her Ukrainian home.

Kalyna, screamed.

Natalka stayed unconscious.

"Hush, my dear. I am a friend of your daughter's, who deeply admires her self-sacrifice. Children are wonderful, are they

not? And, actually... nobody can hear you."
— said the old man, chuckling.

Kalyna screamed again.

The forest ignored her.

"Hush, hush, my dear. I will not stay long. Here — take this seed — it will make your daughter well again... please, persuade her to eat it."

The old man grasped Kalyna's hand, and put the seed into her palm.

Kalyna screamed for a third time.

The old man vanished.

Next morning, Natalka was unable to get up, and Kalyna knew that Natalka could not live until the evening. Clutching at any hope, however brittle, and remembering the strange housebreaker's words, Kalyna made Natalka eat the seed... and — miraculously! — Natalka immediately got better.

Mother and daughter lived together a while longer.

Someone else's child stayed unborn.

THE OLD MAN AND THE YOUNG MOTHER

A teenage Kreutern girl, called Adama, fell pregnant by a tourist known only as, *Jimi,* who gave a false address in Acapulco, and vanished. Adama's parents had died in a car accident some years earlier, and Adama lived in the family house with her older sister, Eva — though Eva was away, working as a chambermaid in the village of Lauffen. Because the sisters had no other family they were very close, and only argued about money.

Having a baby is never as easy as conceiving one. When her little boy was born, the baby's constant crying drove Adama crazy.

What precious few, smart clothes, Adama had, were soon stained with baby's sick. On the occasions Adama visited Bad Ischl, she gazed at the expensive dresses in the shop-windows and felt trapped.

Adama imagined the world outside Kreutern to be a glamorous Eden, bursting with more lovers, rock music, designer interiors, and fashionable clothes, than her village would ever muster. She loved designer interiors, and had magazines full of pictures that made her own home look shabbily dated. Her little boy, Abel, was a leaden anchor, chaining Adama to

Kreutern. Adama often phoned her sister to see if Eva could help financially. Even with generous tips, Eva, earned nowhere near enough to help Adama, so Eva usually ended such calls with a derisory snort.

Adama went to walk off her frustrations in the Zimnitz.

As ever, Abel had to accompany her in his hand-me-down pram. It was the evening of the Summer Solstice: the birds were twittering, the trees were green, the sky was sunny and warm — and, Adama hated all the merry cliches with all her unmerry heart.

Abel started crying — not just whimpering, but howling like it was the end of the world — and the birds fell silent, or flew off. Adama's patience was exhausted. Adama yelled... "If you don't shut up right now, Abel, I'll leave you here. I'm sick of you!"

Adama noticed an old man, dressed in what seemed to be a unisex, white designer smock, standing by the small grey cliff called *the Trefferwand*. The Trefferwand perpetually dripped with water, and marked off the side of the mountain from the path above the rushing Zimnitz stream.

Some trick of the light, made the old man appear to glow. The old man sonorously addressed Adama... "Good evening, my dear. What a lovely little boy! Why are you yelling at him? Some people would do anything, to have such a child. I would love to be gifted a little boy as sweet as yours."

Adama replied by bursting into tears. Then, she poured out her troubles, not knowing why she was telling them to a stranger, and not caring.

The old man listened, and nodded occasionally to express sympathy.

"I will help you, my dear." — said the old man. He took out an enormous gold key, which he stuck into a keyhole-shaped nook in the cliff.

He turned the key.

The mountain creaked open, revealing a gleaming hall, with a ceiling supported by golden columns. On the ground inside, lay every conceivable type of sparkling jewellery, gold coin, and precious stone, piled into heaps that were collapsing under their own weight.

"Take whatever you like, my dear," — said the old man — "and come back for more, if you want. You can stack it up outside."

Adama was so overwhelmed by the situation, she never questioned what was happening, nor who the old man was. All Adama saw was riches and her own escape from Kreutern. She gathered as much treasure as she could carry, and took it outside. She piled it high in the long grass, briefly turning her back to the old man. Then, she went to fetch more.

The rock face had shut.

Adama stared at the cliff, and at the glistering water dripping down it in the twilight — and was unsure, if she was awake, or dreaming. The gold was still there in the grass. Abel and the old man were gone.

Slowly, Adama realised the enormity of what had happened. She began to knock on the wet cliff face, more and more frantically, until her hands were bruised and bloody. Adama desperately searched for another entrance. Adama screamed Abel's name.

Adama was found in the Zimnitz Wilderness two days later, unable to speak, except for huskily whispering *Abel,* over and over again. Adama was accused of losing her son, selling, or even killing him. Her trial was deferred, until she had been psychologically evaluated and received psychotherapy.

Some children playing hide-and-seek, found the treasure Adama left in the long grass. It turned out to be very ancient and valuable, but was donated to a museum despite this.

A wise stranger put a little statue of the Madonna and Child into the Trefferwand's keyhole, to ward off evil. Old women, who know about these things, still bring flowers and light candles there, to protect mothers against the child-snatching envy of the old man of the Zimnitz.

THE CURIOUS RECEPTIONIST

Peter was not tall, short, fat, thin, young, old, stupid, clever, ugly, or, handsome — he was average, and wore glasses. Peter was also curious. So, he worked as a receptionist at the *Dämmerungshof* near Bad Ischl. However, this should not imply that he busied himself with mundane work. Peter's curiosity was reserved for dreams, gossip, and old fairy tales.

During working hours, Peter preferred to read, or looked out of the window at the dense, green forest above the bed-and-breakfast. Peter had been here for thirty years. He was a treasured piece of furniture, though some found his historical patina off-putting.

Peter was responsible for the steady decline in visitors to the bed-and-breakfast, but his boss, Mr. Wurst, blamed the guests for not knowing their place, and for being too infected with the unconvivial efficiency of the big city.

As often as anyone could be bothered to visit, a guest would arrive to find only a shinily arid reception desk. Peter would be sitting out the back, engrossed in a book of local tales — occasionally, even in *Verschlungen.*

Peter had read myths for such a long time, and retold them so often, his mind

was bursting with fantastical beings —
there was no room left, for fantasising
guests and their touristic fantasies.

An annoying, foreign youth called Jimi,
was the only guest currently residing at the
Dämmerungshof. Peter did not like hippie
types like him, who pretended to be from
Acapulco, and who came creeping in after
staying out all night smoking dope at
Castle Wildenstein — or anywhere else, for
that matter.

Peter made it clear to Jimi, that Jimi
was tolerated only because of Peter's
exceptional patience. Jimi would be out on
his ear, if he ever whined about slowness of
service. Peter had more important things to
attend to. He was very keen to meet the old
man of the Zimnitz, and hoped this mythic
spirit would share some of his treasure
with him.

It is not that Peter wanted money so as
to be able to leave his hometown, or his
job, for a better life... he simply wanted
proof of the old man's existence, to impress
the drunken doubters at his favourite bar.

Peter saw treasure only as a means of
buying more drinks, to fuel the admiration
of his acquaintances for himself.

It was nearly home time.

Peter, sighed, shut his book, and
finished work, satisfied that he had read
three long chapters and no guests had
disrupted his concentration. He put on his
blue *Janker* jacket, and decided to look for

the old man of the Zimnitz, as he always did on his way home, before going to his local to gossip about it.

The night was clear, and reflections of the Moon and stars bounced across the River Ischl, as Peter set off deeper into the Zimnitz Wilderness. Sometimes, gravel crunched beneath his footsteps, and sometimes, earth dully thudded. The river gushed more loudly at night, and the trees swayed to the rhythm of its throbbing bass.

When Peter reached Pfandl village, the streets were empty. Only dim, electric light, showed him the way into the darkness of the forest.

Peter strode on, past the traditional Alpine houses, with their wooden balconies and colourful window box flowers, past the forest graveyard with its burning, red grave lights — ever deeper into the Zimnitz Wilderness — towards the Trefferwand, which is said to be the entrance to the kingdom of the old man of the Zimnitz.

Despite the clarity of the sky, and the brightness of the noisy, perfumed forest, it seemed to be taking Peter an age to walk to the Trefferwand. Peter began to doubt his own knowledge of the woods, and thought he might have taken a wrong turn.

A blaze of lightning illuminated Peter's surroundings, and a crash of thunder rang out. Peter stood alone in the middle of a wide market square, in a town he had never seen before.

Old-fashioned town houses, luminously painted in pastel colours, with ornate, decorated facades, and high, square windows, framed the empty, cobbled square. Opposite Peter, stood a massive cathedral, more beautiful than any he had seen, with a gold, zigzag-patterned roof and arched, stained-glass windows, depicting the story of Jesus in an Alpine setting. Light shone out of the church. Peter could hear hymn-singing and organ music.

Peter listened — and, as he listened, the old man of the Zimnitz crept up behind him, and clasped Peter's hand.

This was nothing like the meeting Peter had imagined. The split-second of lightning seemed frozen forever. Peter was as scared as a rabbit is by car headlights, and wanted to cry out, but the old man of the Zimnitz put his heavy finger to Peter's lips. He pulled Peter across the square to the cathedral, the iron gates of which swung open at their approach.

Peter and the old man of the Zimnitz entered the candlelit cathedral, which was as deserted as the square. The music and the singing stopped. Only the eternal flame flickered by the altar.

The old man of the Zimnitz pointed towards a heap of gold coins in the far corner of the cathedral. Silently, the old man gestured for Peter to take some treasure. Peter took a deep breath to master his own fear. Peter was determined to fix every amazing detail of this night in his memory, so he could tell his drinking pals everything that was happening.

Peter examined the painted wood sculptures of the Stations of the Cross: Christ's face had been so well finished that it seemed flesh and blood. The Roman soldiers too, appeared to be breathing. The crowds jeering Christ were so life-like, their cat-calls more disturbing for being silent. The blessed Virgin cradled Jesus' body with all the grief of a mother, and real tears seemed to flow from her image.

It took Peter some time to reach the gold, but, when he finally bent down to pick some up, he became dizzy and fainted.

Peter, lay on the track next to the Trefferwand.

A single candle burnt underneath the statue of the Madonna and Child in the *Keyhole*. It was still night. Peter was cold, and could not understand how he came to be here. Despite having no gold, Peter felt thrilled to have met the old man of the Zimnitz, and was bursting to report it.

When Peter arrived at his usual haunt, breathless and eager to tell his tale, the bar was shut. So, Peter went home.

The next day, the Dämmerungshof too was lifeless and locked up. Peter went into Bad Ischl to try and find Mr. Wurst. People stared at him. A woman Peter had known since childhood, saw him on the Tauber footbridge, and screamed so loudly Peter almost fell over.

Ten years had passed in Peter's absence.

Friends of Peter, thought he was a ghost. To other people, it did not matter how long he was absent: the Dämmerungshof never had many guests.

THE OLD MAN AND THE STUDENTS

A computer science student, Hannes Schlosser by name, returned to Bad Ischl from Salzburg University, to spend Christmas with his parents and his student colleague, Mwangi Njeru. Like most of his species, Hannes had weaknesses for heavy drinking, homemade rituals, and pranks.

Hannes was a chubby, freckle-faced youth, who did not take life too seriously. He read stories about the old man of the Zimnitz online, but saw in them only an excuse to indulge all his weaknesses at once.

On Christmas Eve, Hannes set off with Mwangi into the snowbound Zimnitz Wilderness. Mwangi Njeru was Kenyan — a tall, skinny, youth, with an intelligent face that made him seem more serious than he was. Hannes insisted, they take some holy water from the church of St. Nicholas for protection, and — vitally — a bottle of precious Adlitz Schnapps, to oil the hinges of the evening's entertainment.

Hannes, knew that at solstices, and on Christmas Eve, humans are supposed to be able to enter the realm of the old man of the Zimnitz (so the *Verschlungen* website claimed). He had no idea if this was true, but messing around in the snow might be fun.

The night air was hard, dark blue, and sharp. Myriad stars dazzled. The forest was at its most silent this time of year. The branches drooped with white. The water, which usually dripped from rock faces, was frozen and mute, suspended in midflow.

Hannes and Mwangi, crunched on through the snow."I hope this is going to be good." — said Mwangi, shivering — "Your Alpine voodoo seems a bit fake. And, it's too damned cold to get properly drunk outdoors."

"Have some Schnapps. It'll be fine." — soothed Hannes, who knew nothing about anything, but always prophesied good things.

Neither of them was expecting much to happen, except, perhaps, for not seeing any bears, wolves, or jackals. Yet, when Hannes and Mwangi reached the Trefferwand, there was a weird, misty light illuminating a fresh hole in the rock-face.

Mwangi was later interviewed about that night's events for local journal, the *Ischler Rundschau*, and said — "We stared at that opening but we'd already had a bit to drink, so we weren't nervous — we weren't anywhere near as nervous as we should've been. My friend, Hannes, says: *Let's go in, and see what's down there.*

"So, we climb in, and find ourselves in a narrow passageway blasted straight from the stone. It was surprisingly bright. We followed the passage round a bend, until we reached an enormous, lofty cave, studded with giant, dripping stalactites.

"The cave was divided by a wide, shimmering river, that disappeared into cliffs on either side, and which seemed deep, judging by the smooth, slow flow of the water. There was an old-fashioned salt-barge navigating it... the kind that looks like the lovechild of a coffin and a gondola, steered by two, black-cloaked, masked and hatted, boatmen.

"Damn this for work, Flo! — shouted one of them.

"It's only until we cook up this batch. — replied the other... *We can retire then."*

"I had no idea what they were on about. Hannes and I, noticed the mysterious boat carried a heavy cargo, not of salt... but of heaped gopher corpses, the fur of which glistened in the weird light.

"My first thought was we'd stumbled on some gangsters smuggling drugs inside of dead animals — but then, I wondered, why gangsters wouldn't just use a motor launch, instead of the antique they were in? Either way, the boat was soon out of sight.

"On the opposite river bank, sat twelve scary men at a horseshoe-shaped wooden table. They'd identical red, shaggy hair, and beards — their emerald eyes, blazed with seriously bad intentions. Their coats were a dirty scarlet. At the foot of each man, lay a massive, chained, black dog — like a Doberman, but bigger — with glittering, equally emerald, eyes, and misted breath.

"Either Hannes, or me — I think it was me — realised, there was something odd going on. The twelve men, might be the twelve bringers of evil I'd read about on some old website... each dog was a month of bad luck, ready to tear into people when they least expect it.

"The dogs were tethered because the year was effectively over. Come New Years Eve, I was sure they'd be off their leashes.

"Anyway, I cough. The dogs turn their emerald eyes on me, whine, scratch the ground, and pull at their chains. An old man, wearing what looks like a nighty, with long, white hair and a beard down to his waist, strides in to see what's happening. I know this because he loudly shouts — *What's happening, my dears?*

"The twelve men, being bringers of evil, stay silent.

"*Of course...* slurs Hannes, drunkenly — *It's the old man of the Zimnitz, checking on what's spooking the dogs!* I hush Hannes, but it's too late. The dogs go crazy, barking and straining against their chains until their muscles pop. The twelve bringers of evil, swivel their blazing gazes towards us.

"Scared, I duck behind a rock.

"Hannes doesn't need to duck, because he's

already fainted.

"We really have to get out of there, so, I frantically slap, Hannes, splash holy water on him, and pour the Adlitz Schnapps down his throat.

"Finally, he wakes up.

"I peer over the rock. The men and the dogs are gone. They must be hunting us.

"Hannes and me, run out of that place faster than I ever thought possible. We belt down the narrow passageway, skidding on the ground, tumbling back out into the snow and the open air — expecting, any instant, to be shredded by black dogs. (We never see the dogs chasing us — but then, you never see bad luck until it catches you.) When we get out, the church bells are striking one o' clock... then, the mountain slams shut behind us.

"We are alone in the forest."

Editor's note: *This interview, is part of a longer feature on student drug-taking and alcoholism. It was meant to warn young Ischlerites against the hallucinations caused by heavy Schnapps consumption. Hannes and Mwangi, returned to their studies after a month in rehab.*

THE WIMMER ALM

Above the Zimnitz Wilderness is the *Wimmer Alm:* juicy, green high pasture, onto which, young cows on the verge of producing milk, are moved for Summer grazing. The profession of *Sennerin*, or, milkmaid, which involved a young woman living on the Alm with the cows to guard them, milk them, and make butter and cheese in situ, is defunct. This defunct pleases everyone: the cows, get to wander around by themselves, bellringing for tourists, and, young women spend their summers in the valleys... which suits their lazy lovers sitting in the valley bars very nicely, thank you.

You reach the Wimmer Alm by walking into the forest from Kreutern, following a pounded earth,root-gnarled, trail, uphill through the tall pine trees. Adama often walked here because (she said) she enjoyed being alone. Her appetite for the great world had withered since Abel's disappearance — to the point where her sister, Eva, worried about Adama shunning human contact.

Time often loses its way in the Zimnitz, and events linger in the shadows here long after they happen. Sometimes, even a chronological sequence of tales goes out of order.

So, it was unsurprising when Adama — thinner, but still surprisingly sane after psychotherapy — bumped into the same fairy tale on the Wimmer Alm, as Traudl, the long-dead Sennerin.

Adama prayed that, one fine day, she might persuade the old man of the Zimnitz to return her boy. Adama felt a deep, wrenching undercurrent of longing for Abel, whenever she explored the rocks and trees around her home: every gap in the rock-face, every grassy hill, or mossy erratic, might hide the entrance to the old man's kingdom. Adama lied to Eva — and to herself — when she said that she wanted to be alone. Adama longed to stroll with Abel.

It was a fine day of the kind Adama prayed for, so she wandered up to the Wimmer Alm, searching for any sign of the old man of the Zimnitz. Not finding him, Adama rested wearily on the grass, and dozed off in the Sun.

The cows stared curiously at Adama as she slept. The crickets were still chirruping, and the birds singing, when she woke.

Adama groggily propped herself up on her elbow, scanned her surroundings, and noticed, a large hole had appeared.

Her heart tightened.

She jumped up, straightened her dress, and went to look in the hole.

Amazingly, there was a spiral staircase inside the hole, cut into the mountain: surely, this had to lead to the realm of the old man of the Zimnitz?

The stairs, like the walls, were smooth, shiny, and polished grey stone. It was obvious to Adama, the old man of the Zimnitz is an accomplished interior designer with a leaning towards minimalism.

Adama felt her way along the wall, and made her way down into the mountain.

At the foot of the stairs, Adama entered a large, subtly illuminated hall — another triumph of sophisticated interior design. The lighting source was ingeniously hidden. The hall was carved out of the fashionably understated, grey stone of the mountain. Familiar-looking piles of glittering jewellery and gold coins, were artistically arranged on the ground, their de-luxe, scatter-gun gaudiness, offset by the perfectly flat rock-face.

Now Adama seemed about to encounter the old man of the Zimnitz, she was unsure what she would say to him. Perhaps, she would open by complimenting him on his design skills?

There was a kerfuffle behind Adama. As she turned to look, terror squeezed her heart.

Snarling and baring sharp teeth, a huge, black dog, with poisonously emerald eyes, charged towards her. The dog was so intent on Adama's blood, it tripped over the treasure, and fell down, quickly scrambling back onto all fours in a spray of gold coins. The dog's guttural barks shook the cavern.

Adama knew, the best way to deal with an angry dog is to stand still and look down, but... a terrified inner voice, screamed at her to run. She tore up the staircase, the angry dog snapping at her heels.

Faster — faster! — Adama felt the dog's hot breath on her calves. One of the dog's fangs, grazed her left Achilles' tendon, and...Adama escaped to the surface.

She ran out onto the grass, anxiously glancing over her shoulder.

The dog stopped at the top of the spiral staircase, stared at Adama, snorted, and trotted back down. Maybe, the dog was satisfied with the scratch it had given her — maybe, it knew Adama already had enough bad luck — or maybe, it just did not like daylight.

Adama collapsed on the grass. When Adama looked back at the hole, the hole had gone.

Dejected, Adama walked home.

The evening was warm, and leaves twinkled in the sunlight. The Zimnitz stream, rushed and splashed on. Tree branches creaked in the breeze, like they were stretching to limber up. Crickets strummed contentedly, and birds, trilled... all to confirm, they were happy to be alive.

This joyous music deepened Adama's gloom. She noticed a small fire in her way, perhaps left over from a marshmallow barbecue by children.

This was the final straw!

Adama could not pass it without leaving the trail — and the fire was glimmering, rather than burning brightly — so, Adama, decided to vent her frustration by stamping it out. But, Adama was so angry, she felt compelled to grab some hot embers. She needed to give physical expression to her feelings, and scorch herself until it hurt.

Adama put her hand in the ashes, and clutched the hottest, most orange, cinders.

There was no pain.

Adama withdrew her hand in shock, and opened her fingers, to discover... a piece of gold. She grabbed a glowing fragment of wood, and the same thing happened. So, she grabbed another, and another...

Adama carried on, until there was so much gold she could barely hold it. But, Adama wanted pain, not gold, and continued to scoop up the fire more and more obsessively. Only the total exhaustion of the flames put an end to her mania.

Maybe, the gold was compensation from the old man of the Zimnitz, for having taken Adama's child? If so, it meant nothing to Adama, who saw Abel behind every stone of the mountain, and heard him in every twitch of the undergrowth.

And, giving her compensation, meant very little to the gold-laden, old man of the Zimnitz, who stayed just as he was, when and where he was.

There is no reason for the events of that afternoon: they belong to a tale from another time, which got lost in the forest.

Traudl the Sennerin, faced the same story a couple of centuries earlier — but, she only lost a cow to the mountain, not her son. She was delighted to accept the gold in compensation.

THE NAUGHTY DOG

Despite having no idea what happened in the last decade, Peter found a job in the reception of an Ischl hotel. His local historical knowledge, and his extensive experience as a receptionist, were qualification enough, despite his ignorance of current trends.

Peter energetically resumed reading, sleeping, and gossiping, diligently fighting off all intrusions by guests seeking help.

The hotel's profits did not nosedive, because Peter's interests now included a dog, who was more popular with visitors than Peter was. Unlike Peter, the dog was always attentive and polite, sniffing and licking every millimetre of every individual from face to buttocks.

Peter's dog was a bushy-tailed, black, white and brown, husky cross-breed, with staring golden eyes and super-canine energy. Like the old man of the Zimnitz, the dog just was what it was, when and where it was.

At work, his dog's hippie behaviour was perfect for Peter, but during walks in the forest, it was difficult to tell which end of the leash was in charge of the other. Peter appeared even less in control of his dog than he was, because he had named the dog, *Husky* — so, Peter always sounded like he had forgotten the dog's name.

Certainly, *Husky* liked to pretend, his own name had nothing to do with himself, whenever Peter struggled to pull him off a deer's scent.

"Husky!" — shouted Peter, despairing of getting his own way. Husky ploughed on, dragging Peter behind him through the undergrowth, barking, as if to say... "Husky? What husky? My name is Friedrich II, Graf von Hohenzollern."

Peter disdained the smug owners of obedient dogs he encountered — no matter, how much their pitying *"Grüss Gotts!"* stung him. Peter was proud of his dog: Husky's disobedience was never disobedience as such, but "t*he untameable spirit of a noble beast.*"

One sunny day, Husky was dragging Peter into the woods as usual. It was coming up to lunchtime, and Peter had been reading a particularly exhausting chapter describing the *Welische Männchen* (a race of little people that appeared in the Zimnitz Valley centuries ago, which spoke a garbled pidgin German called, *Kauderwelsch.*)

Husky shot off into the trees, oblivious to his human pendant. He seemed more excited than usual, sniffing out the trail of some wild animal, or ghost, cleaving through the herbs and grasses like a furry battering ram.

Peter stumbled and lurched behind Husky, trying to avoid all the angry nettles, bushes, and roots, in his way. There was no point in doing anything else: only Husky can stop Husky.

Husky stopped himself by a huge, gnarled tree. Its green leaves gleamed high above, blocking out the sunshine.

Molten gold welled from the tree's black trunk. This was unusual, even for the most exciting of the local plants. Some gold was dripping into a heavy stone cup by the roots, and some stuck to the bark.

Astonished, Peter looked more closely, and — as he did so — let go of Husky's leash, to tentatively touch the gold. Peter forgot, how truly uninterested in precious metals dogs are, despite occasionally expressing a polite interest to please their owners. Husky remembered very quickly — and bolted.

Swearing, Peter hurled himself into the forest after his dog, yelling — "Husky!" — over and over again to no effect, apart from annoying two talking blackbirds.

Panting and wobbly-kneed, Peter finally caught Husky, high up a steep mountainside. Which is to say, he did not actually catch him: Husky's leash snagged on thorns.

Husky barked at Peter, as if to say... "What kept you?"

Tutting at his dog, Peter untangled Husky's leash from the undergrowth. Exhausted, man and beast, trotted back down to the miraculous, gold-leaking tree.

The cup had gone.

Pitch ran down the trunk where there had been liquid gold. Only a glittering speck of gold on Peter's finger, proved that he had not imagined everything. Despite his own, blazing ambition, Peter was no good at prioritising supernatural treasure.

And anyway, his dog did not care for it.

THE LITTLE WELISCHE MAN

Peter was as asleep as you can be, without being dead. He slumped, face down on the hotel reception desk. A string of drool joined his mouth to the shut, leather-bound, hotel guestbook. His snores rattled through the hotel, battering the tick-tocks of the stately, antique grandfather clock into defeat.

Husky dozed on the floor — though, one golden eye opened every now and then, to check Peter was not sneaking off for a walk in the forest without him. The reception radiated a contentment any sensitive visitor would prefer not to disturb.

Little Welische people are not sensitive.

Welische are too diminutive to be shy. They have to shout loudly to make their way in the world, or just to make their way to a supermarket for food. Sometimes, they even have to kick shoppers in the ankles, to clear a path for themselves. Then, a Welische vanishes into the crowd before anyone notices them... leaving some hapless shopper to take the blame for their ankle hackings.

A kick from a Welischer boot, made Peter's big oak desk, tremble. Peter mumbled in his sleep. Husky barked, leapt up, and padded over.

Husky sniffed and licked the new arrival's face, which was exactly the same height as his own. The new arrival, not a tall man, punched Husky on the snout, and shouted... "Getten offen me, you wetten doggen! Hello! HELLLOOO! Waken uppen, sirren. Getten offen, stupid doggen! HEELLLLOOOO!!!"

Peter sleepily opened an eye, and looked — and looked — and, saw... nobody.

A copper coin pinged off Peter's spectacles, drawing his gaze downwards, to the front of his desk. He just about made out a very small, blurred shape, wrestling with the, equally blurred, Husky. The small shape held the dog, and the dog's slobbering tongue, at arm's length, and yelled — "At lasten, somen servicen! Isen thisen your stupid doggen?"

Peter straightened his disordered spectacles, so he could see what was going on. The kicking, shouting, and pinging, shape, looked like an aggressive, bearded little fellow, with sparkling emerald eyes, dressed in a nineteenth century frock coat, embroidered, long leather trousers, and shiny black boots.

Amazed, Peter realised that he was looking at his first, genuine, little Welische. Peter was excited, even as the Welische blustered... "Wellen? Getten doggen offen me — nowen! And taken me to Trefferwand. Dalli, dalli, please!"

Peter stood up, stretched — then, picked up Husky's leash, and shook it in a meaning fashion.

Husky spun round towards him, barking and wagging his tail in readiness for a walk. Peter attached the leash to Husky, and tied him to the desk. Husky was so shocked at this outrageous deception that he physically deflated, staring at Peter in silent, disgusted disbelief.

Peter turned to the mythological little man, with all the dignity a hotel receptionist can muster, and politely asked. .. "How can I help you, SIR?" Peter emphasised the word "sir", as he always did with the more compact male guests to make them feel respected.

The Welische adopted Husky's aggrieved expression, and reiterated — "Taken me to Trefferwand! Dalli, dalli, please! I given you gold." Then, the Welische flicked another coin — gold, this time — at Peter's nose.

"Ouch!" — exclaimed Peter, as the coin bounced off his nose, onto the floor. He stooped, picked up the coin, and bit it to check its authenticity.

"Wellen? Hurry uppen! I not haven allen century!" — shouted the little fellow, as he jigged impatiently from side to side.

Peter grandly dismissed Husky's anguished gaze with a wave of his hand, bowed to the Welische, and took his Janker off its hook. He thrust his arms flamboyantly into the sleeves. Then, he placed one of his hands — suddenly, pleasingly large — onto the Welische's shoulder, and ushered him out of the hotel.

.. "Please, SIR — if you would be kind enough to accompany me, I will show you the way to the Trefferwand. And please forgive me, SIR, but, how much did you say you would pay me?"

"I not sayen nothing. Getten handen offen shoulder — DALLI, DALLI!" -— replied the Welische gentleman, and impatiently shrugged off Peter's hand from his shoulder. Peter retracted his hand, still revelling in its relative largeness.

The unlikely pair walked to the Zimnitz in silence. Peter could not help casting sideways glances at the incey-wincey man. The Welische groaned, whenever he caught Peter staring at him, until he finally snapped... "Stoppen looken at me — dalli, dalli, sirren!"

"Sorry, SIR." — replied Peter, deferentially, continuing to stare at his little companion. They were entering the forest now, and its branches glittered green against the red evening sunlight. The tarmaced road had given way to gravel and earth. The Zimnitz stream, gurgled fitfully nearby, depleted by a long Summer.

They reached the Trefferwand.

"This is the place you seek, SIR!" — said, Peter, portentously, and gestured at the rock-face with his (relatively) mighty hand. The Welische, saw the small statue of the Madonna, and the offertory candles by the mountain's keyhole, and knew that Peter was telling him the truth. He took six gold coins out of his pocket and handed them to Peter, with the words... "Thisen more than enoughen, now getten lost! Go on — dalli, dalli! Leaven me alonen, sirren!"

Peter had so many questions, but knew from his reading, that exhorting a Welische to change his mind, was as useless as wringing blood from a tiny pebble. So, he bade the Welische goodbye with a pat on the shoulder that made the little man glare, and quietly walked away.

When Peter was sure those sparkling, angry, emerald eyes, were no longer looking at him, he darted behind a tree. Peter hugged the tree close, to hide the outline of his body. He watched, as the aggressive little fellow drew back his leg and kicked the Trefferwand.

The mountain, resounded as if it were a gong. Then, the Trefferwand slowly creaked open... Peter, held his breath, hoping the old man of the Zimnitz would step out.

And step out the old man did.

The old man of the Zimnitz, looked as impressive as ever: his long beard and white nighty fluttered in the evening breeze, reflecting the pink dregs of sunlight that clung to the mountains. He carried a huge sack, exchanged inaudible words with his visitor, and handed him the sack. Then, he strolled back into the mountain, whistling, as it creaked shut. The Welische slung the sack over his shoulder with surprising ease, and strode off purposefully towards where Peter was hiding. Anxious now, Peter clung so tightly to the tree its bark dug into his face.

The little Welische man stopped right by Peter, and, without turning his head, called out — "I knowen you theren, sirren! Comen outen! Dalli, dalli — I want to showen you something."

Trying to look nonchalant, Peter shambled out from behind his tree, mumbling — "Oh, sorry. I was just having a pee."

The Welische smiled mischievously at him, and said... "I knewen you were theren all the time. You should haven comen out — I not biten — olden mannen, friendly too! Do you wanten looken innen my sacken? Go onnen! I knowen you wanten."

The Welische put his sack down, opening it a little, standing back and beckoning Peter to peek inside. Peter hesitated. Then, he glimpsed a curious golden shimmer inside the bag, and felt compelled to take a proper look.

Peter walked across, and bent over to see inside.

BANG!

Peter's body catapulted into the air — his coccyx shot upwards, nearly into his neck, compressing all the vertebrae inbetween. His spectacles flew off. Peter, hit the ground, with a sickening, tooth-loosening, CRUNCH.

As he groped for his spectacles, Peter heard the giggle of a very small gentleman, who kicked arses even better than he kicked mountains.

THE HELLHOLE

Lauffen village on the River Traun is famed for its *Hellhole,* but Lauffen is not so bad. A statue of the Virgin Mary even refused to be evicted from the shadow of Lauffen's forested mountain, the *Mountain Of Women.* The Madonna and Child was first found there by a woodcutter and removed to the nearest church, in Goisern town. The wooden Virgin would have none of it, and kept teleporting back to the Mountain Of Women. Which is why Lauffen's, now antique, onion-domed church, had to be built exactly where Her Divine Stubborn Majesty wished to stay, and was named *St. Mary In The Shade.* Which is why the Virgin is still happily ensconced by its altar with her baby. Which is why Lauffen is a destination for religious pilgrimage, despite its hellhole.

Besides its hellhole and immoveable virgins, Lauffen boasts a mill museum, the wild river Traun, and some steep alleys down to the river bank. Lauffen does not boast very loudly. Lauffen's old, stone houses, are large and lonely and unfashionably distressed.

Lauffen's people were nearly wiped out by a plague once, and, on Winter evenings in a local hostelry, you can still imagine what the village looked like after all the inhabitants died. What Lauffen proves, is that Death and Hell thrive wherever religious people gather.

Adama's sister, Eva, liked it in Lauffen — although she was not a stubborn virgin, *Death,* or, the Devil.

Eva did not enjoy her work as a chambermaid, but she did like nosing through hotel rooms to gain a profitable insight into guests' lives. It gave her a thrilling ripple of sin, to imagine the debaucheries that led to the murder of a room she was expected to raise from the dead.

Every now and then, Eva gatecrashed some (thoroughly reconnoitred) male guest, first turning around the DO-NOT-DISTURB notice on the door, to read PLEASE-MAKE-UP-MY-ROOM. Eva would listen for incriminating sounds, arrange her face into a grimace of shocked surprise, then, burst in using her keycard... to catch the guest in a compromising, generous-tip-to-keep-stumm situation.

The current object of her curiosity, was a gentleman in Lauffen to do some hunting. He was a black-haired, neatly bearded, young man, called Mr. Jäger. who dressed in traditional grey and green Alpine hunting dress, with a wide-brimmed, feathered hat. His eyes were a piercing emerald, and never wavered in their thorough examination of people's faces. He had an elegant self-assurance, which always made people think he knew things too important for anyone else to know.

Frustratingly, Mr. Jäger left no clues about himself in his hotel room: no sweets, no cigarettes, no pills, no electronic devices — no trousers, jackets, or shirts. Not even a pair of underpants. Eva was sure, such a fine gentleman could not wear the same underpants for days on end... Maybe, he did not wear underpants at all, because he was a fastidious bather who enjoyed a good breeze?

Eva was fascinated by Mr. Jäger.

Her boyfriend, Gernot, was less keen.

Gernot was in his mid-twenties, brown haired, with regular features and average blue eyes. Despite being considered handsome, he suffered from an inferiority complex since he had always lived in small villages. Gernot was intimidated by visitors, who had seen the world he only studied online. Gernot was obsessed by Eva's reaction to the stranger... because, Eva was a curvy and attractive young woman, who looked like every jaded businessman's fantasy of a bottle-blonde chambermaid. Gernot worried about this, because Eva was also his fantasy of a bottle-blonde chambermaid.

For her part, Eva was too involved in hotel guests' rooms, to worry what others thought. So long as men fawned on her sexiness, she was happy to shrug off the female guests' stony-eyed stares — and, her boyfriend's puppyish anguish.

One day, Eva went for a smoke in the forest. She had just received a voicemail from Adama, urgently requesting money, and wanted to think about it in the soothing coolness of the trees. Eva already knew she did not have the cash for her sister, but felt she ought to ponder this before reaching her pre-ordained decision.

Eva strolled up the *Forststrasse* at the far end of Lauffen, with a comforting cigarette. Unexpectedly, she spotted Mr. Jäger. He was standing near the fork in the road, by the little *Hell Stream,* which splashed merrily through the steep forest, next to that dark opening in the overhanging, limestone rock known as *the Hellhole.*

Water dripped down from above the Hellhole, which was shaped like a small, arched window, and barred by a rusty metal grate, that hung there, broken and useless. Hell Stream was strewn with large, rounded boulders, which made the babbling water vanish into rock pools and shadows.

"Hey!" — shouted Mr. Jäger — "It's a miracle! There I was, just thinking how desperate I am for a cigarette, when up walks this lovely young lady with a cigarette. Please say you've got one for me!"

Eva was flattered.

Of course she had a cigarette for Mr. Jäger! Eva offered Jäger, the open packet. Mr. Jäger pulled out a cigarette, and they sat down on a boulder together. Eva flirtatiously lit his cigarette with hers.

They sat in silence, enjoying their smoke.

Mr. Jäger kept casting sideways glances at her, and his eyes made Eva feel naked... which she did not find nearly as unpleasant, as she might have done with someone uglier.

"Nice day." — said Jäger, between drags on his cigarette.

"Is it?" — said Eva, trying to act cool, as golden sunlight shimmered through translucent green leaves, birds sang tunefully, and the little Hell stream, shimmered on through, ridiculously picturesque, mossy rocks.

Eva sucked on her cigarette, and gazed into some imaginary distance, sensing Mr. Jäger looking at her because of her own, tingling skin.

"Yes, it's a very nice day... a day made for a beautiful woman. Wherever she might be!" — exclaimed Mr. Jäger, cheekily.

Eva registered Jäger's comment as flirtatious, She took a self-consciously cool drag on her cigarette.

"God! Where are the beautiful women?" — sighed Eva, teasingly — "I don't know."

She turned to look Mr. Jäger in the eyes.

He had vanished.

Suddenly, Eva was a popped balloon.

She gathered herself up, and flicked her cigarette stub into the stream, in a defiantly anti-social, public gesture of littering. Then, she stepped across the rocks, back onto the *Forststrasse*, all the while hoping, Mr. Jäger, would leap out from behind some tree and yell,,, "Boo!"

He did not leap out.

Mr. Jäger had not appeared by the time Eva reached the end of the forest. Swearing to herself, Eva stopped on the main road into Lauffen, to light a consoling cigarette.

When Eva opened the packet, she noticed a gleam next to her three remaining cigarettes. Puzzled, she tipped the packet upside down, and discovered a pearl bracelet inside.

Mr. Jäger must have secreted the bracelet when he took his cigarette. Eva's antagonism towards Jäger, evaporated like dew. Eva lit her cigarette, replaced the bracelet in the packet, and walked home, humming happily.

By the time Eva got to the hotel, she was exhausted. Eva shuffled up to her room, threw her clothes off, dived into bed, and instantly fell asleep, clutching the pearl bracelet in her hand.

Eva dreamt of Mr. Jäger sitting on the boulder with her, of his smile and his emerald eyes. She dreamt that she was naked — apart from her packet of cigarettes, which she offered to Mr. Jäger over and over again, and which never ran out of cigarettes, no matter how many he smoked.

And Mr. Jäger... offered her pearl jewellery, again and again. Eva's skin tingled in her sleep, even more than it had that afternoon.

And Eva felt naked, and Eva enjoyed being naked, and Eva awoke — to discover that she really was naked.

Her duvet had slipped off the bed.

Sleepily, Eva looked at the bracelet in her hand, but, as the pearls glinted in the light of the Moon, they turned to water. Eva was not sure if she was awake, or dreaming. Yet, her hand was wet and the pearls had vanished.

Eva picked up the duvet to cover herself, and fell asleep again. She hoped the pearls would reappear when she was properly awake.

The next morning, even the wetness in her hand had gone.

Eva felt irritated by the bracelet's dissolution — but, liked the frisson of Mr. Jäger being interested enough in her to play tricks.

She resolved to scold Mr. Jäger.

It was barely dawn, and Eva was too sleepy to bother answering the messages on her mobile. Eva was not even interested in the rooms she made up that day. All she thought about was Mr. Jäger, and how best to respond to his practical joke. By 10 am. Eva had finished work for the morning. She sat down in the staff smoking area, with a cup of coffee, lit a cigarette, and checked her messages.

A text from Adama, asked Eva urgently to phone her. Eva ignored it, because she did not feel like discussing money before lunch. She did not feel like discussing money at any other time either. She went back to thinking about Mr. Jäger, sipped her coffee, and puffed on her cigarette. Gernot, came to see her, to be needily affectionate.

Eva's greeting to him was frosty. She was not disposed to indulge anyone this morning, and, anyway, Gernot had already been demoted from boyfriend, to over-friendly boy. He just did not know it yet. Eva was not in the mood to talk to him, nor to feel sorry for him, nor to do anything other than be dismissive.

Gernot, left.

Eva stubbed out her cigarette. Once the coffee woke her up, Eva realised she was in a bad mood. She thought of Gernot and her lip curled. Eva knew that she was being nasty to Gernot for no good reason, but this only made her feel more annoyed with him.

Gernot had gone, but, somehow, Eva felt guilty about his absence, which annoyed her even more. Eva decided to use her bad mood positively. She phoned Adama, to tell her there was no hope of a loan.

Adama surprised Eva. Adama was incarcerated for psychological evaluation, accused of losing, or killing, her baby son. She needed money to prove she could subsist, so she would be allowed to go home before her trial for neglect and manslaughter.

Eva was stunned by this, but Eva was still more shocked by the story Adama told her, of a mountain spirit kidnapping Abel. Adama had clearly gone mad. Maybe, she had been unable to cope with having a baby, thought Eva: maybe... Adama, had murdered Abel, and could not face up to the guilt?

All thoughts of flirty practical jokes, financial problems, Gernot, and even Mr. Jäger, were crushed by the weight of Adama's news. Eva was unsure what to do. She was not even sure, she could believe the conversation she just had with her sister.

Eva dragged herself up to go for a smoke in the forest.

Temporarily deaf and dumb, she walked through Lauffen, not acknowledging the people who greeted her on the street, adding to the reputation for anti-social, slutty behaviour, her looks and love of peroxide had given her.

Eva reached the Forststrasse. She sucked at her cigarette as if it were her last. Eva puffed her way through the trees, nervously pacing towards the Hellhole. Eva was oblivious to her Sun-soaked surroundings. She was trying to think, without knowing how, or what, to think.

Hell Stream said nothing useful to her, nor did the breeze.

Eva puffed on, until she reached the Hellhole, where Jäger happened to be sitting on a boulder.

"Hello there!" — shouted Mr. Jäger — "Lovely lady, do you have a cigarette for me?"

Eva was in no mood for Jäger's nonsense, so she emphatically yelled back — "NO!"

Mr. Jäger's face lit up with concern, as he said... "Is something bothering you?"

"Ten out of ten!" — snapped Eva, determined to make Mr. Jäger work for the privilege of sympathising with her.

Jäger slid off his boulder and jogged down onto the Forststrasse, to where Eva was standing. He indulged her... "Please, don't be angry with me. I'd like to help if I may, because I really cannot bear to see such a lovely girl unhappy."

"Really?" — replied Eva, sourly.

"Yes. Definitely. I've a feeling I can help you. Now, what's the trouble?"

This was all the invitation Eva needed. She poured out her conversation with

Adama to Mr. Jäger, who listened intently and never once took his eyes off her.

When she had finished, Eva stubbed out her cigarette, and waited for Mr. Jäger to reply.

"Here, you poor, dear girl, take this." — said Jäger, as he handed Eva a small embroidered wallet... "Open it whenever you need my help. It's got everything inside that you need to call me. Or, just walk up to the Hellhole and yell. I'm usually around here, if I'm not at the hotel. I suspect, I leave a bit early for you when I'm hunting."

Eva was comforted by the reassuring tone in Mr. Jäger's voice... yet, she wondered, why he had not simply exchanged phone numbers, or suggested some solution to her dilemma?

Jäger cut her musings short — "I have to think about your problem — sorry, I mean, about Adama's problem. Come and find me in a couple of hours, please. Until then, could I trouble you for a cigarette?"

Eva smiled despite herself, as she proffered the cigarette. Something about Mr. Jäger, always made her smile, even now... not like Gernot, who irritated her so much that she frowned as she remembered him.

Mr. Jäger took his cigarette, let Eva light it, winked, and strode off, puffing, into the forest.

As Eva wandered back to Lauffen, her gnawing anxiety returned. It occurred to her that calling on Mr. Jäger was no solution to her sister's mental illness, just an excuse to talk to somebody sympathetic. Eva worried about taking time off from work to see her sister, as paid leave from the hotel was never given.

Eva clutched Mr. Jäger's wallet — looking for comfort, which did not seem to be forthcoming, no matter how tightly she squeezed. Eva saw the church looming up, as she walked into Lauffen, and, most unusually for Eva, she decided that she wished — maybe, *needed* — to pray to the Virgin Mary. This statue of a single mother from the Mountain Of Women, must sympathise with Adama.

Before Eva prayed, she would look in the wallet. Perhaps, there was something inside to make her feel better? She opened it and looked, discovering a delicate gold necklace, and an engraved, platinum ring. More of Mr. Jäger's joke jewellery.

Eva put the necklace on... just in case.

She pushed the church door open, and entered. The colourful fresco above the altar, made the Virgin Mary, with her choir and orchestra of angels, look like an old timers' swing band. Unlike the statue, she did not carry her boy while performing. There was a wall of attentive, gold-laden saints on the left, sitting in their framed pictures like a captive audience in its boxes. The Virgin wore a showbiz smile, and had her arms extended wide, as if inviting applause, or going: "Ta-da!"

Eva stopped to stare at this publicity shot of the blessed Virgin, rather than at the Virgin's statue. And, while Eva stared, her gold necklace began to melt, until there was only the faintest feeling of damp left on Eva's neck.

"Ta-da!" — went the blessed Virgin on the ceiling, as though she had performed a brilliant magic trick.

Eva did not applaud.

She left the church in a huff.

Mr. Jäger had gone too far! But... reflected, Eva, maybe, just maybe, Mr. Jäger had not meant to play another joke on her.

Maybe, he had simply forgotten the wallet contained left-over magic tricks? Eva could not believe, Mr. Jäger would deliberately play more jokes on her — not, after he had listened so sympathetically.

Eva opened the wallet again, tipped it upside down, and shook it. The ring fell into her hand. Eva put it on her finger, and examined the engraving, rubbing it with her fingertip.

The sky turned grey-black. The air began to rush and whistle. The old, heavy trees, creaked and shook. Billowing clouds of drizzle blew down the empty street, obscuring the houses, and long trails of fog enveloped Lauffen, whirling through the air like giant serpents.

A bang of thunder, made Eva jump and swear under her breath. No sooner had she cursed, than Jäger appeared, striding towards her through the fog and drizzle, which parted respectfully before him.

"Don't worry, Eva!" — said, Mr. Jäger, jauntily... "I've sorted Adama's money out. She's back home in Kreutern. I haven't managed to find Abel, but I believe Adama's story. If you promise to come and see me at the Hellhole with some cigarettes, I can take you to see Adama. I've cleared your work with your boss. Alright?"

Eva was overwhelmed by his cheery confidence. Suddenly, she trusted Mr. Jäger completely. Yet, she did not know why she trusted him.

Mr. Jäger spread his arms out, and wrapped Eva in his embroidered green overcoat. Eva, gasped, as the storm blew... and she realised, Jäger was riding on the air with her.

When they alighted in Kreutern, Adama was indoors in bed, staring at the ceiling. Mr. Jäger waited outside, while Eva tried to talk to Adama. After kissing her impassive, rigid face, Eva was uncertain that Adama even recognised her, and started to weep.

Wiping away tears, she returned to Mr. Jäger, who spoke gently to her... "I can make Adama well again, and I'll do my best to find Abel. But, you must promise me, you won't pray, or go to church for at least eight days, before you come to the Hellhole to see me. And — make sure, you bring me more cigarettes. Can you promise me that, Eva?"

Eva never went to church much, so this was an easy promise to make. Yet, Eva had to ask Jäger — "Why?"

Mr. Jäger grinned, and replied... "I honestly don't know *why*. It's just what I'm supposed to ask people that I help. Also, I've never liked the soapy, scrubbed smell that churchgoers carry around with them, and I'm not too fond of that stubborn swing band leader, with her childish habit of dissolving my stuff around Lauffen. And, I always forget to buy cigarettes."

Eva was not totally convinced by Mr. Jäger's explanation, but she never cared for the soapy smell of churchgoers either: avoiding church, was an easy promise to make.

The only possible difficulty was the high price of cigarettes... hopefully, Mr. Jäger was not such a heavy smoker as to bankrupt her.

Mr. Jäger handed Eva, a small, corked, glass bottle, containing red liquid. He told her to feed two spoonfuls to Adama every day for a week, to cure her mental paralysis. Then, Jäger kissed Eva's hand, and vanished into the darkness.

That night, Eva gave Adama her first two spoonfuls of medicine. Adama, swallowed them without blinking, and fell asleep in her bed, smiling reassuringly, instead of with a blank face.

Hopeful now, Eva went to her own bedroom, where she slept as soon as her head touched down.

The following morning, Adama was more animated, but still had problems connecting with a conversation. The day after, Adama was a little more forthcoming, and she continued to improve, until, by the fourth day, she talked almost normally.

And yet... Eva felt rebellious, despite her own, best intentions. Now that churches were forbidden, they developed a maddening alure. Praying too, became irresistible: on the fifth day, Eva caught herself whispering a prayer after Adama bedded down. Adama screamed, then smashed her own head against the bedroom wall.

Eva rushed in to Adama — who was sat bolt upright in bed, and seemed fine now Eva had stopped praying. Stroking her puzzled sister's cheek, Eva exclaimed — "Thank God... NO! I mustn't."

She did not pray again.

As days passed, and her health improved, Adama started to stroll in the forest, or up to the Wimmer Alm. Eva relaxed enough to leave Adama on her own. But, there was no sign of Abel, and Eva was unsure what to do.

One evening, when the Sun had set over the mountains — while Adama dozed in her bed — Eva picked up a packet of cigarettes, and headed to the Hellhole. The last twilight was fading and no Moon was due to rise. It rapidly got dark.

The stream seemed noisier at night: a living presence in the silent, rock-strewn, wilderness. Hesitantly, Eva rubbed her ring-finger. She had not taken the platinum ring off since she first put it on, and — unusually for jewellery in Lauffen — the ring had not dissolved. She tried to pull it off.

Eva's ring slipped off her finger so quickly she dropped it. The ring clanged like a cymbal as it hit the stones at her feet. Instantly, Mr. Jäger, stood next to Eva, and clasped her waist.

Nervously, Eva gave Jäger the packet of cigarettes, and allowed him to lead her into the mountain. They stepped through the Hellhole, into a huge grotto, and Eva never questioned, why the Hellhole's entrance was suddenly large enough for them both to fit through.

Inside, the walls were platinum, and studded with jewels — so much so, the chamber glittered in the half-light. Steam, rose from a pool of clear water in the depths of the cavern, and, reflections from the water, rippled on the ceiling. The blackest darkness of the cavern, formed into five beautiful, naked servant girls, with platinum skin, who hurried towards Eva, and escorted her to another, smaller chamber. There, they removed Eva's clothes. Everything that was happening, seemed completely normal to Eva, despite not being normal at all.

The servant girls, assisted Eva into the pool and bathed her. Then, they towelled, massaged, and perfumed her. They braided Eva's hair, and dressed her in cool, luminous white silk, and jewellery, until, Eva looked like a peroxide princess of the Underworld.

Only then, did Mr. Jäger approach Eva. The servant girls discretely withdrew at the first whiff of his cigarette.

Mr. Jäger had used the time Eva spent getting ready, to smoke a third of his packet of cigarettes. He was in a relaxed mood. As was, Eva — who liked her exotic, new get-up, and was delighted by her surroundings.

Jäger smiled at Eva, took her in his arms, and kissed her.

"Well..." — he said, "How do you like my humble abode?"

Eva was too impressed to speak. Mr. Jäger knew then, Eva belonged to him.

Mr. Jäger continued to hold Eva, and talked softly... "I'm a professional hunter, it's true — but, I hunt tourists' souls, not animals. That's why I visit hotels. And, sometimes on stormy nights, when I'm bored and need excitement, I lead the Wild Hunt across the sky, to search for prey. But, it's not your soul I'm after.

"I get so lonely in my work, Eva — and neither my souls, nor my platinum servant girls, make me less lonely. I knew the moment I saw you, that you are the girl for me. Are you brave enough to share my life?"

(Mr. Jäger might have said — "My wife, doesn't understand me." — or — "Do you come here often?" — or, even —"You're so cute I want to wear you like a suit." But he did not, so Eva fell for his patter.)

Then, Mr. Jäger assured Eva, Adama would be taken care of, and Eva could visit Adama whenever she wanted. But, oddly, Eva never did want to visit Adama. Enchanted by Mr. Jäger, Eva forgot all about her loved ones.

Soon, the respectable citizens of Lauffen, were gossiping about Eva touting for men in the forest. Eva was said to have given up her job as a chambermaid, to become a full-time whore.

Old women hissed under their breath that Eva had, anyway, always displayed a vocation for this profession. Eva was rumoured to stand by Hell Stream on full-Moon nights, dressed only in a transparent, white gown, ensnaring drunks and other nature-loving ramblers.

Gossip always exaggerates: Eva did not wear a transparent white gown. Now inured to all weather, Eva had become a naturist.

Mr. Jäger treated Eva as indulgently as any pimp can, and provided every comfort that Eva wished. Eva, was shock-proofed against reality by these comforts — and she happily enticed men, stealing their cigarettes for Mr. Jäger, while he snatched their souls.

One evening, as Eva started her shift, she noticed a potential dupe, ambling towards her in the twilight. Eva had just arranged herself seductively by a tree, when she thought she saw something familiar in the man's gait — she could not put her finger on it initially, but, as the man came closer, she began to see the man's face in the dimming sunlight.

It was Gernot, red-eyed and unshaven.

Eva panicked.

Being confronted by someone she personally knew, made Eva self-conscious — and she felt embarrassed to be naked, and she hid behind her tree.

"Is something wrong?" — asked Mr. Jäger, creeping out of the Hellhole behind her.

Nervous, Eva replied... "It's Gernot. You remember, I told you about him? I'm sorry, but I don't think I can do this. He looks so unhappy... I don't know why, but I feel sad for him."

And then, Eva remembered her sister in Kreutern, and dimly recalled, relatives and friends. Gernot's presence had broken her enchantment.

Mr. Jäger's emerald eyes, sparkled angrily in the deep blue air, as he told Eva..

. "I can't stand shitty sentimentality! Just get on with it."

"I'm sorry, I can't do it."

Mr. Jäger glared at her, and growled — "Do it."

Eva started to obey Mr. Jäger, and tried to look seductive, but stopped before Gernot saw her. She could not do it. She refused even to whistle at Gernot, no matter how annoying he was. It is not that she felt proud of having a conscience: Eva, resented Gernot for yet again making her feel guilty.

Mr. Jäger let out a roar, which vibrated the entire Mountain Of Women, shaking even the foundations of St. Mary In The Shade. Then, he hit Eva so hard across the face, she crashed down onto the tree. He picked up an enormous boulder and hurled it at Gernot.

The boulder missed — rolling away harmlessly down the steep slope.

Mr. Jäger roared once more, and gobbed with frustrated fury.

Gernot bolted into the night.

With her face stinging, and breathing heavily, it took Eva a while to form the words, but when she did so, she yelled... "You cowardly pig! What did you do that for? I am going home, right now — RIGHT NOW!"

Eva began to get up.

Mr. Jäger stared at her, the rage still glittering in his eyes. He said... "You are, home — you can't ever return to Kreutern. How dare you insult everything that I've given you?"

Then, he hit Eva again.

Eva started crying. She was so furious that she ignored her tears. She spat back... "If you don't let me go, I swear I'll kill myself before I let you keep me here."

Mr. Jäger cackled.

Then, he scoffed... "Don't you know yet? You can't die! All you will do from tonight on, is get older. You're stuck with me... but, I'm not stuck with you. There's no shortage of beautiful young women in the world. In a few years' time, when I'm enjoying myself with a less sentimental girl, you'll be a lump of mummified meat and bones, somewhere on The Mountain Of Women, and — if you're very lucky — our own, blessed Virgin, might just dissolve you into water, like my other, worn out trinkets."

And, Mr. Jäger laughed in Eva's bleeding face.

And he lit himself a cigarette.

THE GOAT-OF-ARMS

Bad Ischl's coat-of-arms, features a black and white, golden-eyed, mountain goat, called a *gams,* nibbling on the leaves of an ash tree. It is inspired by a flesh and blood gams that wandered into town on a hot, dusty day, centuries ago, when all the worthies of Ischl were in a beer garden, feasting, and debating what Bad Ischl's coat-of-arms should be.

Gamsen are shy — they have to be, because they taste delicious when roasted. It was puzzling to see one trotting into town, with no fear of stout men — nor even, of stout men's hats, plumed with the plucked beards of shot gamsen. Unflinchingly, the gams started munching on the leaves of an ash tree near the worthies.

That a gams chose to feast with them, seemed a tribute to Ischl's harmonious relationship with Nature. The stout worthies adopted the goat-of-arms as Bad Ischl's coat-of-arms. But, there is more to it than that.

Ischl is surrounded by mountains and forest. The ancient tribes, which once inhabited this area, imagined their Universe as a giant ash tree under constant threat from the servants of chaos.

At the top of the ash tree, perches a fierce, titanic eagle, which flaps its wings to create the winds that make weather happen. There is also a naughty, rat-toothed, red squirrel, that devours the tender leaves of the tree's crown, and which scuttles up and down the trunk. The squirrel relays messages between the eagle, and a massive serpent, known as *the Tearer of Corpses,* which is mother to all giant serpents of the same name. This serpent perpetually gnaws at the roots of the ash.

The squirrel is a creator of fake news, who encourages bad blood between the eagle and the serpent — thus, further damaging the tree, because of the two monsters' angry attempts to kill each other.

Our human race, in all its frail glory, weighs down the centre of the ash's foliage, every twig of which is perpetually under attack from deer and gamsen that feast on the juicy, green leaves.

Only luck, prevents the great ash tree of the Universe, from withering under these ferocious assaults — and, one day, luck must fail.

This world will end.

A gams, which is indifferent to humans, and that cheerfully chews on ash leaves, is not the quirky miracle the designers of Bad Ischl's coat-of-arms took it for. The declaration of war against Serbia — that infamous declaration, which sparked the First World War — was signed in Ischl. The gams feeding on those ash leaves long ago, is a harbinger of destruction.

Luckily, no more gamsen have wandered into Ischl since that first one... not until, Peter spotted one, calmly trotting past the Café Zauner on the Esplanade.

Peter sat outside the elegant, peach-coloured, high-windowed café, slurping his iced coffee, and listening to the piano being tinkled. The River Traun's waves blinked and dazzled. The French windows of the café had been flung open, to admit the clear river air and music.

The mountains gleamed and the woods shimmered. And there came a gams, bold as a burlesque dancer, promenading on the street above the café.

There was no breeze, which is why Peter noticed the gams before Husky did. Husky stayed snoozing under the table. Peter, followed the gams down the road with his eyes, as did the other café patrons, giggling, whispering, and pointing it out to each other.

Cycling children screeched to a halt on their bikes, stared, and took photos with mobiles. The gams treated them with the disdain you would expect from an ominous goat.

Suddenly, a Viennese-registered, four-wheel-drive Mercedes — a big, red heap of steel and self-love — raced around the corner from the bridge, skidded, and thudded straight into the gams, killing it instantly, and causing children to start howling.

Adults stood up at their tables, indulging in outrage, shaking their heads and *Oh-my-Goding*. Husky jumped up and barked.

The driver emerged, dazed but unhurt, from behind his vehicle's blood-and-fur-splattered bonnet, frantically excusing himself to shocked locals.

"Typical Viennese driving!" — mumbled Peter, pushing Husky back under the table. .. never realising, how privileged he was to see an evil harbinger squashed.

THE KREUZSTEIN

Long before Mr. Jäger met Eva, he would often fly down the River Traun, from Lauffen to Bad Ischl to hunt souls — because there are more tourists in Ischl. (Tourists are always easier prey than locals.) It is also further away from the blessed Virgin of Lauffen, who, Mr. Jäger never got along with. And it gave Jäger a break from all his, complaining, mummified exes on the Mountain Of Women. And anyway, Mr. Jäger liked getting drunk in Ischl.

Alas, every silver lining has its cloud, and there was one cumulonimbus that spoilt Bad Ischl for Mr. Jäger: St. Nicholas Church. It does not matter, that everyone else who sees the church thinks it pretty fair.

Jäger, hated, the tall, fashionably thin, church tower — particularly the pointy spire gesturing at Heaven like a lecturer's baton. He resented the loud church bells, and could not bear the church choir's singing.

Especially, THE SINGING!

Whenever Mr. Jäger had to fly past St. Nicholas while hymns were being sung, he stopped mid-air, stuck his fingers in his ears, and spat at the top of the tower, with all his mighty lung-power.

One frosty night, Mr. Jäger was riding the swirling air back to *The Hellhole*, feeling a little tipsy and stroppy after hunting souls and swilling red wine all day. Mr. Jäger saw the spire in the starlight, smugly warning of damnation... and, he could not stand it any longer.

More to the point — he would not stand it.

Mr. Jäger simply had to kick the church roof in.

He took a deep breath, coiled his leg, and kicked — and kicked — but, because he was drunk, he only did minor damage.

The more furious Mr. Jäger became, the less damage he did, until he kicked so hard that his foot skidded on the roof, and he tumbled to the ground, with a tough (but fair) bump.

"That'll teach you!" — said the very fat parish priest, who was loafing around by the entrance of St. Nicholas, unusually late after the pubs opened.

The priest, Monsignor Tiso, was more of a cannon ball, than a canon. He sported a strange, dyed black hedgehog bristle haircut, and a perpetually shiny top lip, in an unnaturally smooth face. His emerald eyes were those of a sad bulldog. He was dressed in an expensive, long green, *Hubertus* overcoat, that covered his over-rounded form entirely, right down to the knees of his pricey grey trousers. Tiso, was a self-made man, who had worked his way up from the bottom of the digestive tract of the Roman Catholic Church, to his present high position, as the mouthpiece of a seething congregation.

Tiso was not remotely fazed by flying soul-hunters, because he believed in religion. On reaching pink adulthood, he discovered that he was no longer ageing: he had been preserved like a ham by church incense. It was easy for him to countenance Mr. Jäger's existence.

That bright night, Monsignor Tiso, had been watching Jäger for some time — tutting, every time Mr. Jäger booted the church roof.

"Who are you?" — slurred Mr. Jäger, grumpily, as he got onto his feet.

"Tiso, *Monsignor* Tiso. And you are...?"

"Jäger — *Mr.* Jäger, to you."

"La di da!" — scoffed Monsignor Tiso — "You're very stuck up for someone who's been caught vandalising church property."

"HIMMELHERRGOTTKREUZMILLIONEN DONNERWETTERNOCHOAMAL!" — yelled Mr. Jäger, cursing blasphemously, and examining a bloody scuff on his elbow... "I don't even know why I'm talking to the likes of you. Do you at least have a cigarette, to make up for the shit that's happened to me tonight?"

(Like all the damned, Mr. Jäger is a Narcissist: nothing bad is ever his fault, though everything good is.)

"No." — replied Monsignor Tiso, with a smirk — "I have to save my money for the church's restoration. You know the kind of thing... damaged roof, that kind of thing."

"HIMMELHERRGOTTKREUZMILLIONEN DONNERWETTERNOCHOAMAL!" — shouted Mr. Jäger, a second time.

"Well, if you're going to take that attitude, sir, I'm glad I don't have a cigarette! Do you hear yourself? Are you going to pay for the damage to my roof?"

"HIMMELHERRGOTTKREUZMILLIONEN DONNERWETTERNOCHOAMAL!" — screamed Mr. Jäger, rather hysterically, and flew off.

Monsignor Tiso remained, standing in front of his church — observing Jäger until he was less than a speck of dust in the starry sky.

Mr. Jäger was furious.

He got back to The Hellhole, jumped straight into his hot pool, and was scrubbed by his sparkly servant girls — but continued to pulse with fury. Meeting Monsignor Tiso had sent Jäger over the edge. Tiso, and that eyesore church of St. Nicholas, must go!

Still inspired by wine, Mr. Jäger resolved to dam the River Traun with rocks, to flood Bad Ischl — most especially, to flood out St. Nicholas and drown Monsignor Tiso — teaching Ischl's piety-mongers a lesson they would never forget.

The vision of Tiso being washed out of his church like some panicking beach-ball, made Jäger smile as he dropped off to sleep.

The next morning, Mr. Jäger woke, filled with purpose and joy. He gave one of his platinum servant girls' bottoms a merry pat on the way out, and flew off down the Traun. He searched the mountains around Bad Ischl for the largest boulders he could find, and began to push a suitably huge one towards the Traun. But even with Mr. Jäger's supernatural strength, it took him until early evening to heave the massive rock into the river.

There was a mighty splash, as the boulder hit the water... a splash that did not go unnoticed by a fat priest on his afternoon digestif walk.

Monsignor Tiso enjoyed enormous, fibre-rich, vegan lunches, laced with garlic, and he always belched and farted for a very long time afterwards, like a ruminating cow. Tiso had to walk around to expel all his gas and pre-empt explosions.

Luckily for his parishioners, Tiso, preferred to do this out in the open, where the fumes could disperse without causing offense to the dignity of his office: hence, the digestif walk. Hence Tiso's own little contribution to global warming.

Monsignor Tiso watched Mr. Jäger intently from behind a very wide tree, and, while not having a clue about what Mr.

Jäger was up to, Tiso, was absolutely certain it was no good.

Tiso is a priest. He knows evil.

Mr. Jäger knocked off early that evening, satisfied with the new islet he had created in the River Traun. In Bad Ischl, Tiso got busy on the phone.

The next morning, Jäger was in such a good mood, he merrily patted two servant girls' bottoms on his way out. He whistled a happy tune as he rode the air down to Bad Ischl, to pick up more boulders for his dam.

As Mr. Jäger drew closer, he saw a crowd of people standing on the riverbank by his boulder islet. And, horrifyingly... a big cross, with a golden, crucified Christ, had been fixed to the boulder.

Mr. Jäger's rock, would henceforth be known as *The Kreuzstein.*

Jäger nearly fainted mid-air, and angrily plummeted down.

When Monsignor Tiso saw Mr. Jäger diving towards him and his congregation, he belched, apologised, and started up the choir — "Altogether now, let's dedicate this reborn rock to the birth of Our Lord. *Ave Maria...*"

This was too much for Mr. Jäger. Even sticking his fingers in his ears, could not mute the horrible, self-satisfied cacophony. He let out the pitiable scream of a musical aesthete in agony. He could have pulped every last one of Tiso's singing gang — but, the horror of the music was too overpowering.

Mr. Jäger braked his descent, then — retreated.

Retreating, Jäger momentarily caught sight of Monsignor Tiso's grinning face, as the priest, loudly and tunelessly, led his flock in noise pollution. Mr. Jäger gunned back erratically to Lauffen, cursing and spitting all the way — and, if he had a pet cat, he would probably have kicked it, as he strode into the Hellhole and yelled...

"HIMMELHERRGOTTKREUZMILLIONEN DONNERWETTERNOCHOAMAL!"

THE DWARVES OF JAINZEN

Welische people are not the only little people found in the Zimnitz region. There are indigenous dwarves too. Jainzen Mountain, the smallest, roundest mountain hereabouts, is home to the smallest, roundest, richest people hereabouts: the *Bergmännlein.*

Jainzen Mountain rests on four, towering, solid gold pillars, which the Bergmännlein erected long ago deep under the earth. They guard these pillars even more zealously than they do their other treasures. If anyone ever pulled out the pillars, Jainzen Mountain would tumble down in a heap of rubble.

Bergmännlein are about the same height as a child when it first begins to walk — though a little person, in short, is always as tall as they feel.

The male Bergmännlein grow bushy beards, wear leather aprons over loose white shirts, and carry pickaxes, dangling from the braces of their long leather trousers. They use lanterns, because, despite being nocturnal, they cannot see in the dark. As for the females: nobody has ever noticed any, but some anthropologists have posited they are just like the males, right down to the beards.

A long time ago, Bergmännlein were often seen by locals. On full-Moon nights, the Bergmännlein would go down to Groschen Stream, to wash their shirts and dry them in the moonshine. The Bergmännlein held a Summer Solstice festival each year on the flowering meadow there, and invited any local farmer who could be trusted not to crack jokes about short people.

The human inhabitants of the valley, accepted the Bergmännlein as a part of their world, and the communities of dwarves and humans lived in harmony. The dwarves even offered their own, secret medicines, if a human fell ill.

A world war, and then a civil war, reached out to clutch Jainzen Mountain by the throat. Nowhere near far enough away, a screaming man, with a moustache grown sado-masochistically to imitate his enemies, seized power. Then, he decided that those people who did not meet his long-legged, blond ideal of racial franchising, were scheduled for redundancy.

Strangely, he did not measure up to his own specifications: in his corporate branding, he did not include himself — nor his friends — nor even his friends' friends — nor any other super-aspirational humans that he happened to approve of. Being short and dark himself, the man conceived a special hatred for dwarves.

It was not a good time, especially for the Bergmännlein — and they began to withdraw from human company. Even locals turned against them, now that a second, crueller world war was brewing.

Tiso, then merely a *Father*, was young at the time, but already flabby and inflated with the wind of righteousness. He saw an opportunity to expand his influence under the new regime. Tiso too, cherished a special hatred of the dwarves, who had never embraced Christianity — or Father Tiso. The Bergmännlein were indifferent towards the Church, which meant they were unacceptable to the scathing gazes of the devout.

Father Tiso plotted to seize the Bergmännleins' wealth. Their treasure could be used to ease the war-suffering of devout people — like Father Tiso. It must not be wasted on, quite possibly monosexual — and definitely, godless — dwarves.

On the night of the Bergmännleins' Summer festival, Father Tiso sneaked into action. Tiso was even jollier than usual, as he collected his two, blond and strong, collection-plate boys. The three of them, made their way into the Moon-bright air. They wished to check that the dwarves were distracted enough by their own festivities, to allow three thieves to creep into Jainzen Mountain unnoticed.

A raucous party was bubbling: some Bergmännlein were playing fifes and drums, and some danced the *Schleuniger* conger. Some Bergmännlein had looked too deeply into their jugs of mead, and stumbled through the orchids and buttercups in an alcoholised daze. And some Bergmännlein looked so deeply into their jugs that they fell, face down, to inhale the ground. Other Bergmännlein just lay back and stared at the Moon.

Here and there, farmers and their wives sat chatting with Bergmännlein on the grass — but there were fewer humans than at previous festivals.

One of Father Tiso's boys, noted down the farmers' names and addresses, for the benefit of the authorities. Satisfied, they had found out everything they needed to, the weighty threesome set off for the Bergmännleins' home mountain.

The thieves easily broke down the gate to the interior of Jainzen Mountain. As they suspected, the entire network of shafts and grottoes was deserted.

Father Tiso switched on his torch, blinked, and was instantly bedazzled: they were in the midst of great, glittering, heaps of gold coins and gems. Father Tiso rubbed one of his thighs in glee. His boys unrolled the voluminous hessian sacks they had stashed in their pockets, and opened them out for a rich stuffing.

"This should help a few Christian children enjoy their next Christmas!" — whispered Father Tiso, barely able to contain himself. His curly-haired assistants grinned, like two ewes spotting a gorgeous ram.

Father Tiso wanted to establish the full extent of the Bergmännleins' wealth, so he told his boys to keep their sacks at ease, until they had explored further. The thieves inched forward, deeper into the silence of the mountain's interior, until, at last, they penetrated into the central chamber, where the four gold pillars stood.

For a split-second, the three of them were silenced by the amazing ingenuity of the dwarves. Then, Father Tiso gleefully smacked his lips, and said — "Get your saws out, boys. I'm sure we can get one of these beauties out tonight!"

His chubby, blond boys, started sawing — ignoring, the loud cracks that began to echo through the mountain like splitting ice, becoming more and more frequent, harsh, and scary, rupturing the rhythmic sound of their sawing.

When Tiso's assistants finally heaved the sawn pillar off its base, the mountain began violently to shake, and the ground trembled. Stalactites crashed down from the ceiling, almost impaling Tiso. The mountain listed like an ocean liner in a hurricane.

Terror supplanted greed in the heart of Father Tiso.

"Let's scarper!" — yelled he, at the squeaky top of his voice, and raced off. The three heavyweights were surprisingly quick when scared, and did not stop sprinting until they reached St. Nicholas, where they collapsed in sweaty, breathless heaps.

The next day, Father Tiso gathered up all the religious, racially franchised thugs that he could muster. He equipped them with axes, saws, spades, pit-props, and sacks, and returned to Jainzen Mountain to finish the job.

When Father Tiso's rowdy, blond gang, arrived, the entrance to the Bergmännleins' home, was covered by fresh rubble and soil, and impossible to find.

There was even a new, gurgling spring, welling up out of the earth. Father Tiso was forced to give up. And some of the thugs might have called Father Tiso a liar, or a timewaster — but only under their breaths, because Father Tiso is a man of the cloth.

Nobody saw the Bergmännlein again.

THE WILD HUNT

Jimi stared at the sky. He lay flat on his back, on a wooden bench in Bad Ischl's *Kurpark,* and studied the storm clustering above him. Mighty, black and grey clouds, were whispering to each other, throwing the odd teasing raindrop down to attract any hurrying pedestrian's attention.

The clouds were becoming balled fists, ready to unleash a hiding on this sunny day. Other people might have been worried by this, but Jimi relished the prospect and gave it his most vigorous approval.

"Wicked!" — sighed Jimi.

Jimi had been looking forward to a really violent thunderstorm ever since he arrived (so long as he did not have to ramble through it). Actually, Jimi had been looking forward to a storm ever since he had seen a promo for the anthemic song, *Blitzen,* featuring his own favourite, heavy metal axe-man, Donner, hairily playing air-guitar on a hotel balcony, while lightning and rain crashed around him. Jimi had completely forgotten the unfortunate incident with the girl-feminist-monster thing at Wildenstein.

Now, Jimi wanted to imitate Donner, videoing himself with his smartphone for his friends' unbridled acclaim.

"WICKED!" — his friends would exclaim, when they saw Jimi's video.

"Wicked." — sighed Jimi, languidly thinking how wicked this prospect was. A raindrop splashed Jimi's nose. "Wicked!" — sighed Jimi, again, with more emphasis, and turned onto his side, exposing his builder's cleavage to the shocked burghers of Bad Ischl.

The sky darkened.

Proper rain hit the town. Gusts of scrapey wind dragged across Bad Ischl, until its modernised, *Fin de Siecle* streets, emptied. Each raindrop was a sharp pinprick, and slowly, imperceptibly, the night converged with the storm and grey turned to black. Forks of lightning jabbed the growling sky.

Thunder rocked the mountains.

And soon, Jimi rocked too.

Jimi had his little speaker on at full throttle, facing outwards from his room in the Dämmerungshof, towards the whipping strings of rain. Jimi's smartphone was propped on a window-sill, recording Jimi, who cavorted on the balcony outside, wearing nothing but a pair of jeans and an ecstatic rock-god grimace. The rain made him feel alive, as he frenziedly fingered his imaginary guitar.

Across the mountains, Mr. Jäger stubbed out his last cigarette of the day, and readied a champing, furious spirit-steed — as did each of his companions, the nine-hundred-and-ninety-nine souls of the damned elite, permitted to hunt for souls across stormy skies until the skies fall.

The Wild Hunt was on.

The Wild Hunt had galloped over Bad Ischl for centuries, riding in from between Wildenstein and Dog's Hill (renamed *Sirius Kogel,* to attract posh tourists), and tearing down into the valley in search of human souls. The hunt then continued on to the towering cliffs of *Traunstein*, where they dumped their quarry's flesh-and-blood shell — or what was left of it.

Sometimes just a leg would be hurled down. It was the only leisure-time the damned were allowed to enjoy, so they made the most of it.

Mr. Jäger gripped his reins and whistled. His nine-hundred-and-ninety-nine fellow riders howled and yodelled, as their mounts reared up and charged into the night. Four-thousand hooves pounded the air — rain, thunder, and lightning, sprayed in all directions.

The hunters were on their way, whooping exuberantly, scanning for prey, with the blazing, emerald eyes of the damned.

Two-thousand eyes fixed on a little electric car below, but ignored it, because the hunters are sticklers for tradition, and carry only, bows and arrows, lassoes, and daggers. Cars are too difficult to attack. Wilder hunters did occasionally try to scare motorists into crashing, by charging directly at them on the road, or galloping heavily over car roofs. But tonight every hunter wanted instant meat.

The Wild Hunt revelled in stormy skies, falling trees, and crashing roof tiles. No hunter would rest, until they had captured, or killed, at least one human. All one-thousand covered the short distance to Ischl in the glance of an eye.

One rider spotted a lunatic on a balcony: the lunatic was pretending to play a guitar in the rain, grimacing as if possessed, and half-naked. The rider hallooed to his companions. Their two-thousand emerald eyes burned up the night. Their four-thousand hooves hammered towards Jimi.

Mr. Jäger swung his lasso down to catch Jimi.

The lasso sliced through the air, caught Jimi's chest, and ripped him up into the sky before he knew what was happening. Jimi tried to cry out, but the tightening of the lasso was so fierce it winded him.

This was nothing like bungee jumping.

Jimi dangled from the screaming skies, unable to see, or hear, terrified and icy cold. Raindrops cut Jimi's face. The Wild Hunt became a mob of cats pawing at a twitching shrew, howling, as they passed Jimi from rider to rider, whirling him above their heads, or scraping him on the tree-tops.

Mr. Jäger cackled, as the hunt caterwauled across the sky.

Finally bored with Jimi, the Wild Hunt discarded him on the jagged, freezing rocks of Traunstein.

Sunrise was sharp and painful for Jimi — though the storm had passed. Every bruised inch of Jimi's skin, hurt — every drop of blood seemed jammed into his overloaded brain. He moved slowly, unable to guess what had happened to him. A lazy breeze went straight through Jimi instead of around him.

Jimi gazed down from the remote limestone rock face, on which he had been left, and could not understand anything that he saw. Even his worst drug-trip had never been like this.

The Sun rolled higher without becoming warmer.

Alpine vultures circled in the valley below.

Some puzzled mountaineers arrived after a long climb. Jimi attempted to talk to them, and to answer their questions... but his larynx had dried up.

The mountaineers were stunned, to find a sunken-cheeked, bald, old man, so high up on the cliff — especially, a bald, topless, old man wearing just jeans. They phoned the mountain-rescue and got Jimi to hospital.

Jimi died two days later, without uttering a word. Because of what happened, Bad Ischl's old peoples' home tightened security — to ensure no confused inmate could ever climb so high, or far, again.

THE PLAGUE

Plague once crept from house to house in the Traun Valley. She was known to be a terrible witch, who softly stole into sleepers' beds to strangle them. Nobody knew if she was beautiful, or ugly... nobody had slept with her and lived.

For their part, the dead always looked ugly in the morning — the puffed-up leavings of a badly misjudged one-night-stand.

There were not enough gravediggers, or hours in the day, to bury all Plague's victims. So people stopped bothering with funerals. Those fleeing from Plague, could stagger a day without meeting anyone living.

Just nine people were left in Ischl, contemplating the scattered, putrefying corpses of their neighbours, too scared to nod off... in case, Plague snuggled up with them. The living stayed alive merely from habit. There were no staffed hospitals, or doctors, and the last herbalist had been burnt for witchcraft the year before. There was no hope — except God, who said nothing.

The nine leftovers decided it was better to risk dying on the move, than wait for Plague to clamp their throats in Ischl. They made the pilgrimage to Lauffen, to beg for aid from the miraculous Virgin of St. Mary In The Shade.

Halfway there, they met the last seven inhabitants of Lauffen. This tattered remnant of humanity had left for Ischl, rather than waiting to be choked to death by Plague in their own village.

Lauffen had suffered worse than Ischl. Lauffen's capricious Virgin was more interested in staying put in the shade — and in annoying, Mr. Jäger — than she was in saving people. One godless person even suggested that the blessed Virgin moonlighted as the plague-witch.

These last sixteen people in the Traun Valley, had lost all their loved ones, and their communities. They were exhausted beyond caring. Wherever they went, Plague had already visited. The refugees dispersed into the mountains and forests, and prepared for death. Their footprints criss-crossed as they looked for somewhere soothing to die.

One of the fugitives, a woodcutter, overheard two blackbirds chatting. And — oddly — he understood what they said, and — even more oddly — they said something useful.

One said... "You must take pimpernel and gentian, whenever you feel sick."

The other blackbird replied, "Oh — thanks for the tip. I'll get some immediately!"

Being religious, the woodcutter believed that only inanimate objects had miraculous powers of speech... so, he thought the talking birds were relaying a message from the Blessed Virgin of Lauffen. He gathered all the pimpernel leaves and gentian roots he could find, and ate them — as did the other survivors, once he recounted the blackbird's words.

There was a mass uprooting of pimpernel, and of gentian flowers, which did their best to hide, closing up whenever the sky became overcast. It would have been better for them if they had hidden when the Sun shone.

Soon there were barely any of the flowers left in the Traun Valley. People got healthier, and even reproduced, until today, when there are far, far more humans... and far fewer wild pimpernels and gentians.

Centuries later, Hannes Schlosser was walking in the forest. Plague had long since retired, to become a brothel madam for younger diseases.

Hannes heard the same two, immortal blackbirds talking to each other. One of the birds coughed, then said, "As I was saying..."

Hannes was not sure if he heard right. He had not touched booze for a year, not since his adventure in the Trefferwand, so he was more confused than he might otherwise have been. He paused under the branch on which the two blackbirds perched, to check he was not going mad. But the chatting blackbirds were as oblivious to passers-by as any human gossiper.

The first blackbird said — "Do you remember, when I told you to take pimpernel and gentian for your psittacosis? And those people suddenly started uprooting all the flowers?"

The second blackbird said… "Yeah?"

The first blackbird continued, "Apparently, they thought the flowers cured plague. They thought, me talking to you was a sign from Her Indoors, for them to pick all those flowers and eat them."

The second blackbird gasped — "They never! Did it work?"

The first blackbird twittered on — "Don't know. It might just have been a placebo, or natural immunity, but… they did get better. I wasn't even sure those flowers cured psittacosis. I just knew they tasted like medicine, and searching for them would take your mind off being ill."

The second blackbird exclaimed — "You are clever!"

Blushing proudly beneath his feathers, the first blackbird replied… "Well, cleverer than that old Virgin in Lauffen, anyway — not that people credit me for it."

He was wrong. Hannes Schlosser thought the first blackbird was very clever.

For a blackbird.

THE STORMBRIDE

In the Zimnitz Wilderness, in that modest bed-and-breakfast named the *Dämmerungshof,* lived, Vroni Wurst, with her perpetually bruised husband, Hans. They ran the place alone since the unexplained disappearance of their receptionist, Peter. Vroni Wurst was a fierce, loud young woman — often bored, always red-haired and beautiful — curvier and taller than her foul-mouthed old husband, who used the word "shit" like an errant punctuation mark. Hans Wurst was a man in his early sixties, who calmly took all the punches handed out by his wife.

It was rumoured the Wursts were hares in human form, because male and female hares, box each other's ears in Spring to test suitability for mating. It used to be thought the boxing animals were bucks, competing for female favour, and maybe they were — once.

In these days of alleged gender equality, it is a battle between male and female — and, female hares only accept those males that can hold their own. Many plucky, over-aspirational males, are beaten down, and doomed to die without offspring by their victorious objects of desire. Such a hare is Hans Wurst.

Vroni enjoyed herself with a succession of hikers. Hans gazed down on the amorous doings of his wife, from the rarefied, snowy mountain-top of his own, advanced age. Everybody knew Vroni only married Hans Wurst for stability. Yet, the Couple seemed a perfect fit.

It may even be that the blows Vroni rained down on Hans, meant she had not rejected him as a sexual partner. She was still testing him out as a potential mate. Hans Wurst continued — firmly — to believe in the old saying: "*Erst Hiebe, dann Liebe*".

One sunny day in the Zimnitz, Mr. Jäger was idly riding the air in his hunter's garb, searching for tourist souls to snatch. He spied the Dämmerungshof in the forest, and descended to take a proper look. The door of the whitewashed, wood-ornamented, Alpine bed-and-breakfast, was wide open, so he sauntered in.

"Hello?" — yelled Mr. Jäger, even though Hans Wurst was standing right there behind the reception counter, in crumpled, tan trousers, slippers, and a holey, grey cardigan.

"Shit." — replied Hans — "I'm not shitting deaf you know! How can I be of service?"

Mr. Jäger grinned. He was not used to being addressed in such a vulgar manner. People usually adored him, or were blind scared. Mr. Jäger was uncomfortable with anything in between.

"Well?" — said Hans, impatiently.

Vroni was listening in the office behind the counter, and swept into view, all cleavage and waving hands, a bossy, pink Dirndl-clad, whirlwind. "Don't annoy our guests!" — she commanded, smiling at Mr. Jäger, as she cuffed Hans on the back of his neck... "I'm so sorry, sir, my husband has no manners. How may I be of assistance?"

Hans Wurst did a little bow — as Vroni had taught him — and withdrew into the office.

Mr. Jäger looked at Vroni Wurst and liked what he saw. "What a lovely young lady!" — he exclaimed, in a stage-whisper, so Vroni would hear him, and think he was overwhelmed by her beauty, despite politely trying to restrain himself — "I wonder, dear lady... could I, trouble you for a cigarette?"

Vroni, was thrilled by this handsome stranger in his immaculate clothes. She quickly found an open packet of Hans' cigarettes in the office, thumped Hans when he objected, returned, and handed them to Mr. Jäger.

Thanking Vroni, Jäger took a cigarette from the packet, and held it out for Vroni to light, which she did — instantly — glad to be the centre of his attention.

As Mr. Jäger took his first sip of smoke, Vroni asked him — "Please, sir... how may I address you?"

"Jäger — Mr. Jäger."

"Charmed! I am *Mrs.* Vroni. Mr. Jäger, can I be so bold as to ask, are you planning to grace our humble establishment with your presence?"

Mr. Jäger took a luxurious drag on his cigarette, smiled, and said — "Are there any other guests staying here? I like to make sure a place is worth visiting before committing myself."

Vroni took out her mobile from her cleavage, tapped it meaningfully, and handed it to Mr. Jäger... "Here, sir — look. We have excellent reviews."

"That isn't what I asked. I prefer my information to be real, not an imitation concocted by money-grubbing tech geeks. How do I know anything online is true? You might have written those reviews yourself."

"I would never do that, Mr. Jäger."

"So, there is nobody staying here? You expect me to be beguiled by the mirages on your handset? If you hadn't kindly given me a cigarette, I would already be gone."

Vroni stared at Mr. Jäger in confusion — as he intended. Jäger liked to mix praise with criticism, to put a girl on the backfoot.

Jäger had already made up his mind: he was going to take Vroni away with him to his Hellhole. He no longer cared, if there were any tourist souls to snatch in the Dämmerungshof. It did not really matter, if he persuaded Vroni to come with him either. Persuasion was just a game Jäger liked to play — revelling in his own psychological insights before kidnapping a girl.

But Vroni is a boxing hare.

Vroni answered back... "Our establishment has not merely got the best reviews of any around here — it has the only reviews of any around here. Because... it is the only one around here. But believe me, sir, if it was one of a thousand establishments around here, it would still have the best reviews, because that is how Hans and I run it. If you wish to stay — please, stay. Otherwise... carry on to Bad Ischl and GOODBYE."

"Shit! Did you call me, Schatzi?" — said Hans Wurst, peering hopefully from the office doorway.

"Nobody called you, you deaf old coot!" — snapped Vroni, rolling her eyes.

Hans Wurst did a little bow — as Vroni had taught him — and withdrew back into the office.

Mr. Jäger finished his cigarette and did not like how things were developing. He was not as in control of this situation as he wished, so he lit himself another cigarette.

"I thought you didn't have a lighter, Mr. Jäger?" — said Vroni, sharply.

Jäger hesitated, then decided he could only go for broke... "Please, don't be angry, Vroni. I have a confession to make. I am not really here because I need a room. I... I hardly dare say it — I heard tell in Bad Ischl, that the most beautiful woman in the area, ran a bed-and-breakfast in the Zimnitz, and I simply had to see you. Call me a foolish, feckless, young man, but I am glad I came to find you. I didn't realise you were married. If only..."

"*If only*?" — interrupted Vroni, suddenly interested.

"If only you weren't married, I would take you in my arms and kiss you." — said Jäger, plaintiffly, relying on his own good looks to paper over the cracks in his logic.

A meaning cough emanated from the office.

"Hans, the beds need dusting!" — shouted Vroni — "You should get them done before more guests turn up."

Hans Wurst shambled out of the office, did a little bow — as Vroni had taught him — said "Shit", and went to dust some beds.

"Well, what are you waiting for?" — pouted Vroni, thrusting her cleavage at Mr. Jäger. Suddenly, she trusted Mr. Jäger completely. Yet she did not know, why she trusted him.

Vroni took Jäger's hand in her's, and led him out into the forest. She preferred to make love outside, among the green trees and scents of pine. It was more convenient for throwing lovers off cliffs.

Mr. Jäger spread his arms out, and wrapped Vroni in his embroidered green overcoat. Vroni gasped, as a storm blew up out of the clear sky... and she realised, Jäger was riding on the air with her. He laughed as he gazed into Vroni's eyes, and whirled her round and round, in an insane, heady waltz that seemed to spin up into the Sun.

Faster and faster they spun, until — confusingly for Mr. Jäger — they stopped dead in mid-air. Vroni's hands clutched him like steel talons.

Jäger did not know what was happening. He was so disturbed that he actually apologised... "I am sorry, Vroni, this has never happened to me before. I must be more tired than I thought."

Vroni said nothing.

She looked straight into Jäger's eyes and shrieked with laughter. Her laugh was so powerful, her breasts nearly broke free from her Dirndl. Her laugh was so loud it scattered cawing crows, and people heard it all the way into Ischl. Vroni's laugh was so unladylike it scared Mr. Jäger, who wanted her to let go of him.

Vroni did not let go.

"My turn!" — trilled Vroni, spinning Mr. Jäger round in the other direction, and whistling up a waltz, as black storm clouds thickened above them. Lightning crackled and thunder banged, as some invisible orchestra, relentlessly and imperturbably, played the Blue Danube waltz by Johann Strauss Jr.

They waltzed upwards through the thunderstorm, faster and still faster, until Jäger was too dizzy to speak. He wished to ask Vroni, who — or what — she was, but his tongue was wedged into the side of his mouth by the g-forces. The air was too thin for him to breathe now.

Vroni laughed as she said... "You have me in your arms like you wished, Mr. Jäger, but where are my kisses? I am very disappointed in you. Next, you will tell me, you don't like waltzing!"

Jäger needed to get shot of this monster — or, whatever she was. He let go with one of his hands — it is not like he was holding onto Vroni anymore anyway — and struggled to draw his *Hirschfänger* knife. He clutched tightly onto its reassuring, carved antler handle, gathered the last remnants of his strength, and plunged the blade into Vroni's thigh.

Vroni screamed.

The invisible orchestra stopped.

Vroni let go of Mr. Jäger, who fell for what seemed like forever, through lightning-filled black clouds, which singed his beard, crashing through the tree canopy, before smashing, head-first, into a rock.

It really hurt.

Dazed, Jäger could not get up again straight away. He scuttled on all fours to hide under a mossy precipice, until it seemed safe to head home to the Hellhole. Mr. Jäger was sure Vroni would recover. Supernatural justice demanded more permanent vengeance. Vroni Wurst was not the only one who could whistle up a storm.

A week later, after his bruises healed, Mr. Jäger gripped the reins of his demonic horse and whistled. His nine-hundred-and-ninety-nine fellow riders of the Wild Hunt, howled and yodelled, as their mounts reared up and charged after him. Four-thousand hooves pounded the air — rain, thunder, and lightning, sprayed in all directions. Behind the hunt, trailed all the monsters embedded in the folds of people's brains through the ages... because they were eager for a good, gory show, and do not get out as often as they used to.

The hunters were on their way, whooping exuberantly, scanning for their prey, with the blazing, emerald eyes of the damned. As ever, the Wild Hunt revelled in stormy skies, falling trees, and crashing roof tiles. No hunter would rest until they had killed Vroni and Hans Wurst. They covered the distance to the Zimnitz in the glance of an eye.

Two-thousand eyes fixed on the Dämmerungshof. Mr. Jäger saw Hans Wurst, taking out bins for the trash collection, being scolded for his slowness by Vroni, who — satisfyingly — was still limping after her encounter with Jäger.

Mr. Jäger, hallooed to his companions. Their two-thousand, emerald eyes burned up the night. Their four-thousand hooves hammered towards the Wursts. Mr. Jäger, swung his lasso down to catch, Vroni. His companions cackled and jeered, as she sidestepped his pass. Red-faced, Mr. Jäger had another go.

"Do something, you old coot!" — yelled Vroni, at her husband, as Mr. Jäger bore down on her.

"Shit!" — exclaimed Hans Wurst, leaving his slack jaw hanging open. He took a deep, anxious breath, and sucked down the entire Wild Hunt, with all its champing, demonic steeds and monstrous hangers-on, into his stomach.

Hans burped.

"About time." — said Vroni, rolling her eyes.

"Shit! I've got a shitting tummy ache now..." — groaned Hans, "What the shit shall I do?"

Vroni shrugged — "Do what you always do after a big meal. You don't need me to tell you."

Hans Wurst sighed, and shuffled off to the lavatory, where he deposited Mr. Jäger and the Wild Hunt. After being flushed down the pan, treated in a sewage works, and washed through various rivers into various lakes, the, ferociously cleansed, Wild Hunters — now feeling very sorry for themselves — wearily reassembled on the Traunstein, before heading home to Hell.

Hans and Vroni Wurst were never hares, boxing or otherwise. He is the Zimnitz mountain, who takes every thing his

stormbride wife can throw at him, no
matter what damage she does.

Trees are uprooted, rocks crash down,
flash-floods pour out of him, but Hans —
the Zimnitz mountain — just is what he is,
when and where he is. He does not lose his
temper, even when Vroni dumps her latest
spent, dead lover in one of his canyons.

Given what happened, Mr. Jäger
thought it a good idea to make friends with
the Wursts.

THE STUMBLE ROOT

Mwangi Njeru has never believed in invisible Kobolds. He is a student of computer science, who only believes in things he can see — or which he has been told exist by reliable sources. How he knows these sources are reliable, never having met them — nor, having seen them write their scientific papers — is an easily solved conundrum.

That is what University is for: to authenticate the information students are fed, so they do not waste time questioning what they gulp down.

Being a sober, educated man, Mwangi is now so rational he does not believe what happened, to himself and Hannes Schlosser, in the Zimnitz last Christmas. Hannes is not sure it happened either.

That is what sobriety does for you.

Nonetheless, because of his own rustic heritage, Hannes still believes in Kobolds. Mwangi was staying with him at Hannes parents' house in Bad Ischl for the Summer, when they had a friendly spat. Mwangi wanted to go for a walk in the forest before lunch, but Hannes was busy writing an essay for his course, so Mwangi said he would explore by himself.

Hannes glanced up from his computer, and said — "Alright, but be back for lunch. You know my mother panics if we're not on time. Stick to the trail and don't get lost. You never know what Kobolds are lurking in the Zimnitz, waiting to mislead you."

Mwangi laughed... "Kobolds? Really? I've got sat nav on my phone, and an Internet connection. Mwangi, one — Kobolds, nil."

"Don't be so sure about the Internet, Mwangi... the Internet is all Kobolds. Just because you can't see them, doesn't mean they won't mislead you."

"I don't believe in Kobolds." — snorted Mwangi.

"You certainly do believe in Kobolds! You do computer science, don't you?" — exclaimed Hannes, enjoying the argument more than composing his essay — "Every time you go online, you're talking to Kobolds — even flesh and blood people become invisible Kobolds in the Metaverse. You only guess, who, or what, you're communicating with. Our forest Kobolds are like that: nobody has ever seen them, but everybody sensible knows they are there."

"Kobold, Schmobold!" — said Mwangi, putting on his sneakers.

"Please yourself." — sighed Hannes, returning to his essay.

Neither of them suspected there was a Kobold in the room with them. The Kobold was as bored by Hannes' essay as Hannes was, so he decided to follow Mwangi outdoors, even though Mwangi did not believe in him. The Kobold had no idea what a "Schmobold" is either, but knew it must be a slur, and was duly offended.

As Mwangi and the Kobold set off from Ischl towards the Zimnitz Wilderness, it was a bright, clear morning, and rays of sunlight pinged off the River Ischl. Sometimes, gravel crunched beneath Mwangi's footsteps, and sometimes, earth dully thudded. The recently rained-on river, gushed loudly, and the green trees swayed to the rhythm of its throbbing bass.

When Mwangi reached Pfandl village, the streets seemed empty, but were actually filled with mischievous, chattering, Kobolds.These greeted Mwangi's Kobold, who had by now worked himself up into frothing outrage about being called a *Schmobold.*

"This bastard called me a Schmobold!" — complained the Kobold — "He needs to be taught a lesson."

"Schmobold? That's racist!" — said another Kobold, as the Kobolds nodded and muttered angrily. None of them had heard the term "Schmobold" before, but they all somehow knew, Mwangi was beyond the pale.

Oblivious to his own unconscious bias, Mwangi strode past the traditional Alpine houses, with their wooden balconies and colourful flowers, past the forest graveyard, with its burning, red grave lights — ever deeper into the Zimnitz Wilderness. The Kobolds danced and jogged around him, climbing up trees, nodding and winking at each other from behind bushes and stones. Having been bored most of the morning, they were now enthused with malice.

Ignoring Hannes' advice, Mwangi immersed himself in the woodland, away from the gravel-strewn trail, shadowing long patches of moss into dense trees, stepping over dark, tangled, tree roots. Before Mwangi knew where he was, he was nowhere at all. Mwangi was intoxicated by the forest. The whispering trees were so fragrant, and the springy mosses so soft underfoot,

"Boot a root,

Bumble and grumble,

Three days stumble!"

… chanted the first Kobold, casting a spell that turned every root into a stumble root.

A *stumble root* is the enchanted root of a tree, and if anyone touches it with their foot — they will not recognise anything they have seen before, no matter how familiar. Ramblers stumble around for three days before the spell expires. Some ramblers even die of exposure, and are gathered up by Hans Wurst.

"That'll teach him to call us *Schmobolds*!" — said the Kobold. Tittering, the other Kobolds held their breaths, waiting for Mwangi to step on a stumble root.

Mwangi looked at the time on his phone and saw it was getting close to lunch. He opened the sat nav, to make sure he took the quickest route back to Hannes. The phone's mechanical voice started telling him which way to go. Staring at the map on his phone, Mwangi strode off.

"That's cheating!" — said Mwangi's Kobold.

"What do you expect from someone who calls us Schmobolds?" — snapped the Kobold next to him.

Suddenly, it seemed like the Kobolds were not going to have any fun at all, let alone, avenge themselves on Mwangi. They did not yet know, how evilly enchanting mobile phones are.

Mesmerised by his screen, Mwangi failed to notice his surroundings. When he hit a stumble root, Mwangi did not merely tap it with his foot: he tripped over the root, twisted his ankle, and banged his head on a tree. His mobile phone smashed on a stone.

"Big dog's cock!" — yelled Mwangi, thinking nobody could hear him. His uncouth language merely confirmed the Kobolds' low opinion of him.

Gleefully cheering, the Kobolds concluded mobile phones were not that bad. "I need to get me one of those!" — said the first Kobold — "Imagine, how much mischief we could make, hypnotising people with them."

Mwangi got to his feet, picked up his broken phone, straightened his clothes, and set off further into the forest. Thanks to the stumble root, he lost mastery of his feet. His limping steps did not head back to Hannes' house, but carried him higher and higher up into the cliffs and trees. Nothing Mwangi saw, registered, even if he passed it ten times.

The Kobolds followed Mwangi for a while, but quickly got bored when he did not fall off a cliff. They descended back on Pfandl, to find someone more entertaining to be outraged by.

All afternoon, Mwangi wandered like a stranger, trapped inside his own perceptions, seeing nothing as it really was. The gnarly trees and knotted roots, glared at him with twisted, grinning faces — the rocks frowned — the grass and flowers tittered malevolently.

Every thing was, at once, exactly like every other thing, and nothing like any other thing. Every thing seemed out to trick Mwangi. When night fell, it made the world still more threatening. But Mwangi could not stop rambling, and sunrise did not lift his confusion.

At noon, Mwangi stumbled upon the front door of Hannes' house... wherever that was, and whoever it belonged to. Outside, there was a parked police car — whatever that is — and, two uniformed men, chatting to a strange woman. When she saw Mwangi, the woman screamed... "There he is! That's Mwangi!"

The police officers, turned, and strode purposefully towards, Mwangi. Terrified, Mwangi had no inkling of who the screaming woman was, let alone of his own name. Nor did he know why these two stern men were trying to catch him.

Mwangi ran for it, but was unable to run.

Mwangi limped and hopped.

Mwangi did not get far, because the police officers were very quick for police officers. Mwangi was caught and taken to hospital. Since he could not recognise Hannes, or Hannes' mother — nor even give his own name — Mwangi was tested for psychedelic drugs.

Nothing was found, so Mwangi was prescribed psychotherapy once he recovered his mental faculties, a day and a half later. His therapist uncovered numerous brain conditions that do not exist except in the minds of psychotherapists. Therapy extended the time it took Mwangi to recover by six months.

Mwangi has no idea what happened to him in the Zimnitz — yet, he is still wary of the Internet, and has never said *Schmobold* since.

There is no illustration here, because Kobolds refuse to be filmed, photographed, or drawn. You will just have to imagine one.

THE FROSTY MILKMAIDS

Near the summit of the Dachstein — or, *Roof Mountain* — a glacier, blazes white in the sunshine, where once there was juicy, green high pasture, inhabited by happy cows and skipping milkmaids. The reason the milkmaids skipped is because they had so little work to do, and were too given to yodeling, singing, and clapping. The cows were happy because they themselves were born congenitally deaf, and did not have to listen to the milkmaids' wild partying. The deafest, least disturbed cows, always produced the most milk, so, by the time of this story, natural selection means every single cow is stone-deaf and laden with rich, delicious milk.

So much food was too easily produced by the frolicsome milkmaids — acting on behalf of very underpaid cows, and, the occasional doomed pig — that the girls became very, very, wasteful.

They drank freshly distilled, warm Schnapps, instead of cups of tea. The path leading to the drinking fountain was cobbled with truckles of cheese. Gaps in the walls of their wooden chalet, were mended with cuts of the finest ham. They shined their shoes with butter and bathed in double cream.

The Dachstein milkmaids believed they were entitled to luxury just because they were Dachstein milkmaids. Any exhausted, hungry traveller, who happened upon their chalet, would not be given a crust of stale bread and butter, nor even, a glass of sour milk, because — whoever they were — they were clearly not a Dachstein milkmaid: their skin was insufficiently creamy, and their shoes were never shiny enough.

A hiker might make their way to the chalet, treading on truckles, to find, dancing, piping, singing milkmaids, skipping and giggling all over the place. The doe-eyed, brown cows, would be happily chewing some of the best pasture on the planet, oblivious to the non-stop chalet party. Looking forward to food, drink, and a good time, the delighted hiker would stop and stare.

When the milkmaids noticed the hiker, one of them — usually, big, red-eyed, Rosi, who was fat and jiggly despite all the skipping and dancing — would race over, and demand — "Who are you? More to the point, *why* are you?"

The other skipping milkmaids would pause, titter, and go back to skipping around.

Big Rosi, bigger than the tallest hiker, would fix her gimlet gaze on the hiker's face, and sternly announce... "I hope you aren't looking for a free lunch — we barely have enough for ourselves."

If shy, the hiker would then apologise, wish Rosi all the best, and continue on their way... to death by exhaustion.

If brave, the hiker might look at the cheese truckles cobbling the path, the sleek, placid cows, the frolicking milkmaids, and say — "You don't look like you're starving... please, can't you spare something? A little glass of milk, perhaps?"

Instantly, Rosi's face would cloud over, and her mouth would thunder... "Are you calling me fat? You horrible little rat! I think you had better leave."

If the hiker did not move fast enough, another milkmaid would fetch two, emerald-eyed, black dogs, to chase the hiker until they fell off a cliff.

And that was that.

Until the last time — when a threadbare, white-bearded, old man, who could barely support himself on his *Alpenstock*, limped towards the door of the chalet. Big Rosi watched him, as he staggered from cow to cow, leaning on each one to catch his breath, before moving on to the next. She did not intercept him, but waited by the door, enjoying his efforts.

"Oi! Stop dancing a second — and come look at this old fool. He's hilarious!" — yelled big Rosi, to the milkmaids.

Reluctantly, the girls stopped piping and skipping, and came over, striding past the old man as he collapsed on another cow.

The milkmaids joined Rosi by the door, nudging each other, and giggling, as they watched the old man struggle towards them.

When the old man finally reached the door, Rosi eyeballed him frostily, in her usual fashion. The other milkmaids tried to keep a straight face, as he plaintively asked... "Dear ladies, please, could you spare a crust of bread and some milk for an old man down on his luck?"

Big Rosi puffed herself up to her full height and girth, and snapped — "Go away, you silly old fool! Do I look like I'm made of bread and milk?"

(She did, actually.)

The other girls laughed out loud, as the old man shrank back and trembled. But, then... he started growing bigger and bigger, until his shredded, ragged clothes, barely protected his modesty. He towered over the milkmaids. His mighty beard billowed in Rosi's face, as he chanted in a deep, resonant voice that made every girl's ribcage vibrate...

"You have spurned the Dachstein king

Ice shall freeze your kine and kin

A glacier will bury you and all your herd

No thaw shall free your curdled curd!"

Then, the King of Roof Mountain took three titanic steps and was gone.

Snowy storm clouds, gathered overhead and burst open — a chilly wind blew — and millions, maybe billions, of snowflakes, flurried wildly around the chalet, stinging the milkmaids' faces.

Big Rosi and her gang rushed indoors.

It did them no good.

Their dogs ran away. The cows are icy blocks now. The chalet is crushed and buried forever under a huge sheet of ice, with all the frosty milkmaids frozen inside. This punishment is a bit harsh on the cows, but there you are. When it comes to people, the King of Roof Mountain is more caring. He strongly believes in prisoner rehabilitation.

On Rauhnächte, the milkmaids are allowed a conjugal visit by the Wild Hunt. This unleashes a drunken sing-song, skip, and dance, on the Dachstein glacier, to oil the rusty cogs of intimacy. And, because she works in hospitality, Vroni Wurst often visits, to offer her expert advice on how the imprisoned milkmaids should treat guests in future... if, they are ever released from the ice.

Big Rosi finds Vroni Wurst very boring. After Vroni's lectures, she is glad to return to her own icy damnation. It turns out: being frozen rigid, is not nearly as bad as being lectured.

THE SAINT IN ST. WOLFGANG

St. Wolfgang is a tall, wiry, perma-tanned man, with a passion for well-made, navy Italian suits, and sunglasses. His raffish *designer stubble* is very popular with ladies of both sexes, and he is a pathological flirt — though, being a saint, he has never gone further than a chaste kiss.

Otherwise, St. Wolfgang is fairly typical for a saint, in that he is always hanging around and refusing to decay. He claims to prefer his identity be kept secret, yet seems delighted to let clues to his identity slip. He has never bothered to move house, nor even to travel, choosing instead to extol to visitors the delights of St. Wolfgang lake, St. Wolfgang town, and, of course, St. Wolfgang church. He is employed as a tour-guide.

One afternoon, sunlight was bouncing merrily over the waves of the lake, and the mountains were dark blue pediments, supporting a radiant, cloudless sky. St. Wolfgang was in his electric launch, cruising on the water with a group of tourists, telling the tale of how the famous, gleaming white, lakeside church of St. Wolfgang, came to be built.

"Long ago, on a hot day just like this one, St. Wolfgang was guiding a group of pilgrims to the little church on the Falkenstein, which some of you visited yesterday. The town and the church of St. Wolfgang didn't exist yet, and the lake was called something else too... because, I'd only just arrived in the area.

"Anyway, it was a beautiful day when they set out in their boat. And... I'm not saying it was God's doing, and I'm not saying it was the weather, but there was something weird going on, because a terrific storm blew up in the clear sky. The raindrops came down like bullets, and the lake quivered with the impacts. Our pilgrims' little boat was bumped by waves, like it was a walnut shell, and the panicking pilgrims feared for their lives.

"St. Wolfgang stayed calm.

"*Listen* — said, St. Wolfgang, ignoring the storm — *God's just like you. He's quite fair: if you make Him feel good about Himself, He'll feel good about you in return. He only gets upset if you ignore Him. He wants to feel loved, that's why He created us in the first place. So, if we make Him feel loved, perhaps He'll let us live a bit longer? We'll build Him a church right here as a thank you, if He lets us survive this tempest. .. What do you say?*

"Some pilgrims wailed, some turned green, and some vomited. But, I could tell they all agreed with St. Wolfgang — and, suddenly, an enormous wave picked up our boat and rushed it towards the shore. And that wave didn't smash us on the rocks like we expected, but put us down softly on the land, thanks be to God.

"The pilgrims stumbled off the boat, too dazed to comprehend what had happened. St. Wolfgang took the initiative — and reminded them of the promise he'd made to God on all their behalfs. As the rain died down, St. Wolfgang marshalled the sheepish pilgrims into work gangs, to start building a church. He told them to gather rocks. Grumbling under their God-given breaths, the pilgrims, obeyed.

"St. Wolfgang wasn't only a saint: he was a born leader, a talented architect, and a brilliant site manager. But those pilgrims... well, some of them were only five years old, and some were over eighty, and they weren't the best builders. No matter how sweetly St. Wolfgang encouraged them, progress was slow. So, being a sympathetic sort of saint, St. Wolfgang told them all to sit down.

"Then, St. Wolfgang strolled off into the forest. He said he was looking for firewood, but really wanted a private word with Lucifer about progressing the new church. You see, Lucifer was an old friend of St. Wolfgang's, and he lives everywhere at once — though, Lucifer can be grumpy since his promotion to Devil-in-Chief.

"Some of you are wondering how St. Wolfgang can be friends with Lucifer? You mustn't forget, God and the Devil are both in the soul business, so it's unsurprising saints and devils meet at cheese-and-wine parties to swap tips. After all, it's how St. Nicholas and Krampus got together.

"Anyway, I'd met Lucifer at a couple of parties where he'd been the guest speaker, and we usually get on like a Hell on fire. But today, Lucifer was in one of his grumpier moods. His first words to me were — *What do you want?*

"No — *How do you do?* — or — *Pleased to see you, Wolfie, old boy!* But I knew, beneath his gruff manner, Lucifer is a conscientious worker and a bit of a pussycat. God's older and lazier, so, if you want something doing quickly, you should always call on Lucifer first. And anyway, we couldn't very well ask God to build His own church for Himself, when we were building it to thank Him for saving us.

"I explained to Lucifer that I'd made a promise to Himself Upstairs, to build a church in His honour.

"*And are you sure, it was Himself that saved you?* — quibbled, Lucifer — *It wasn't just one of those chance events?*

"Well, the truth is, I wasn't sure how we got saved... but I do like to make sure that I'll get saved in the future. It was important to me to build that church, in case I got into trouble again."

One of the tourists — an annoying, speccy, little American fellow — coughed... "Excuse me for interrupting, sir, but why do you keep on saying *I, me,* and *our,* when you actually mean, St. Wolfgang?"

St. Wolfgang knew how to deal with this type of backseat detective.

"It's because I really am St. Wolfgang!" — said St. Wolfgang, and winked. The tourists laughed so much they almost tipped the launch over.

Nobody suspected St. Wolfgang of being St. Wolfgang now that he had admitted to being St. Wolfgang. St. Wolfgang continued. .. "I said to Lucifer: *Listen, Lucy, the pilgrims aren't really up to building a church, so I was wondering, if you could just, maybe...*

"Lucifer raised one of his manicured hands, to quieten me. Then he said: *Now, Wolfie, old boy, I'm a skilled professional, and I only use the very best workers and materials — which doesn't come cheap. If it were up to me alone, I'd help you in an instant... but there's my demons and imps to consider. I can't make them work for nothing. They get little enough thanks for doing Himself's dirty work in Hell, without doing freebies for saints.*

"I couldn't deny that Lucifer had a point, but I wasn't about to undermine my negotiation by agreeing with him. So I played it cool, and said: *What do you think it would take to keep your workers happy? And remember, we saints aren't made of money.*

"Lucifer loudly sucked in air through his whitened teeth, then said: *Very tricky, Wolfie, old boy. Devils, can be a stroppy bunch, if they feel they're being taken for granted. I tell you what... you give them a new soul to kick around in Hell, and we'll build you your church. Just let them have the first soul to enter the church when it's finished. Can't say fairer than that!*

"Lucifer was right. One soul is a small price to pay for a first-class church. The only problem was: how would I break it to the pilgrims? Which of them was going to give up their soul?

"*Come on, old boy* — said Lucifer, impatiently tapping his Gucci-shod foot — "*Don't look a gift-horse in the mouth!*

"I agreed to Lucifer's proposal, though I wasn't at all sure any of the pilgrims would sacrifice their soul. *EXCELLENT!* — exclaimed Lucifer, and vigorously shook my hand. He went off to collect his work gang, and I strolled back to give my pilgrims the news."

St. Wolfgang paused, waiting for a response from the tourists.

"Well, go on then!" — said a raucous, sunburnt blonde, from Croydon, England.

"Alright, madam... I found my pilgrims drying off on the lakeside — some had even hung up their hair shirts to air. I explained the situation to them, and we decided to draw lots to see whose soul was going to be gifted to Lucifer. We cut some identical lengths of reed. I put a thorn inside the hollow of one, and we mixed the reeds up for our draw.

"Meanwhile, Lucifer and his builders darted about — as efficient as anyone could wish for. The imps and demons worked so quickly, they became a humming blur, impossible to see with the naked eye. The only way you could tell devils were at work, was that the church kept growing.

"The pilgrims picked a reed each, but were shaking before they'd even examined the insides. One of them, a pretty young girl engaged to be married, actually screamed — and fainted.

"She'd found the thorn.

"The pilgrims glared at me in disgust... like they'd forgotten, it was me who ensured their rescue. I read the first line of a murder mystery in their eyes, and knew my name might not be on the last page. People are so sentimental about young lovers.

"Anyway, I had to say something, before they drowned, brained, or strangled, me. So, I volunteered to be the first one into the church, to offer up my soul as a football for Lucifer's labourers. I hoped Lucifer would remember our friendship and let me off.

"The church was nearly finished, when the young fiancée woke up again — and said that she'd just been to Heaven, where the angels told her she would be married and live happily ever after. No mention of me sacrificing myself, of course! No Divine message for poor, old St. Wolfgang.

"The church was finished, and stood there, like it had been here forever — white and radiant in the Sun, with a black roof, huge square tower, and stubby crayon spire with a gold crucifix on top. Lucifer and his crew were inside, waiting for their payment. The pilgrims' promise, to name, the lake, town, and church, *St. Wolfgang* in memory of me, did not allay my terror about being sent to Hell.

"I knew that Lucy was conscientious, I knew Lucy was my pal, but, I also knew: Lucy can be nasty.

"So, I dragged my feet towards the church entrance as slowly as I could, hoping to think of a way out before I got there.

"Nothing came to me.

"I shambled, and I — shuffled. I walked so slowly, I nearly walked backwards. I was terrified.

"Go on then, Wolfie! — shouted one of the more annoying pilgrims.

"This was it. No escape.

"I was about to put a tremulous foot over the church threshold, when this huge, hairy, black wolf, with eyes like emerald flame-throwers, trotted out of the forest and pushed into the church ahead of me.

"A THUD — a yelp! — and a gust of sulphur erupted inside. Smoke soured the air and soot showered down on me. Pilgrims applauded, as I bravely stepped into my new church with my soul intact.

"I've never seen Lucifer since. That church, the town that grew up around it, and the lake, were duly named *St. Wolfgang* forever — after myself. Himself Upstairs was in a merry mood that day.

"Not only did He save me from becoming Hell's football by sending the wolf, He punned on my name, which means: *Walk Like A Wolf.*"

The sunburnt blonde from Croydon, asked — "How come your mate, Lucy, couldn't tell the difference between you and a wolf? Didn't you used to shave yourself?"

St. Wolfgang frowned, then said... "I think, Lucifer, was in a hurry that day, madam. He can be a bit quick to grab things before he knows, who, or what, they are. He's avoided me since it happened, so he's probably too embarrassed to admit that he might've taken the wrong soul."

The tourists stared at St. Wolfgang, who was haloed by the glittering sky, and none of them was impressed.

They were forced to listen to more of his tales, and it spoiled their enjoyment of the church, which — St. Wolfgang stubbornly claimed — had been built by devils, and named after himself. When the tourists saw the gilded altar was attributed to someone called *Michael Pacher,* they knew: St. Wolfgang is a liar.

St. Wolfgang, no longer appeared to the tourists as a well-groomed, besuited, ladies man (with a great sense of humour), but as a smug, wannabe gigolo, who talked only nonsense.

This so-called 'St. Wolfgang,' clearly knew nothing about the area — and it was outrageous that he took money under the pretence of being a trained tour guide. He probably did not even have a licence for his launch.

Later that day, when the so-called 'St. Wolfgang,' was mauled in St. Wolfgang town, by a singed, snarling wolf, which mysteriously leapt out of St. Wolfgang church, forcing said 'St. Wolfgang' to jump off the cliff, into St. Wolfgang lake, breaking both his St. Wolfgang ankles, all the blonde from Croydon said, was...

"Serves *St. Wallgunge* right."

THE HEAVENLY PILGRIMAGE OF MONSIGNOR TISO

While drinking red wine in the KuK. Bar in Bad Ischl, Mr. Jäger heard that, Monsignor Tiso planned a little pilgrimage, processing with his parishioners to the church of St. Mary in the Shade in Lauffen.

"HIMMELHERRGOTTKREUZMILLIONEN DONNERWETTERNOCHOAMAL!" — screamed, Jäger's alcoholised brain.

This must not be allowed to happen.

Mr. Jäger hated both the blessed showbiz Virgin, who turned all his cunning enchantments into water while smugly saying *Ta-da!* and Monsignor Tiso, who provoked him with Christian nonsense that he did not himself believe.

(Like every Narcissist, Mr. Jäger knows what is right, and disapproves of people who do not.)

Forsaking his usual hunter's garb, Mr. Jäger donned a pink hoodie, rainbow scarf, red jeans, and white trainers, to disguise himself. He was aiming to look like a teenager in search of an identity. It was a look calculated to appeal to Monsignor Tiso, who (like Mr. Jäger) was always searching for new souls to capture.

Chuckling, Mr. Jäger pulled down the hood and lowered his chin into his scarf, so Tiso would see only black hair and

171

colourful fabric, instead of Jäger's face. Jäger joined the pilgrims milling around outside St. Nicholas Church in Bad Ischl.

A traditionally uniformed, Alpine brass band, played music... of a sort. Their gams-bearded, shaving brush hats, looked splendid in the sunshine. Monsignor Tiso, was dressed in his ornate, church rig and cassock, glittering in the bright light, surrounded by a worshipful congregation of fans. Flanking him, stood his two, grinning, blond and strong, collection plate boys — as miraculously ageless as himself.

The brass band halted its oompahs.

"Is everybody ready?" — asked Tiso, as his pious followers nodded, smiled, and said yes — "Then... let's go go go!"

The band started up again.

They all set off, marching along the River Traun, shadowing its bank to Lauffen. It was a beautifully sunny day, perfect for a pilgrimage.

Mr. Jäger could not resist jogging up to Monsignor Tiso to tease him. Tiso was already sweating, but smiled benevolently at the pink-clad youth who came up alongside him, and said... "God greet you! You're new to my church, aren't you, my son?"

"I am." — answered Jäger, trying to sound like a teenager — "But I really don't know why I bothered. On a day like this, the world is so beautiful I can't imagine ever wanting to go to Heaven."

"Oh, my son, Heaven is even more beautiful than today is. But, it's good you can see God in His Creation. Because, that is what beauty is... the presence of God. That is why you will absolutely love Heaven when you get there: you will be close to God for all Eternity."

"Crap!" — scoffed Jäger — "If all this beauty is the presence of God, why bother going to Heaven? Do you know, Dad — may I call you *Dad*, Father? — if Heaven was only knee-high to a grasshopper, I still wouldn't bother climbing into it."

"Firstly, young man, I am a *Monsignor* — you may certainly not call me *Dad*. And secondly, Heaven is not knee-high to a grasshopper. I'll tell you somewhere that's lower than a grasshopper though: Hell. You will certainly go there, if you carry on as you are."

"Will you go with me, Father... to guide me?" — asked Jäger, who was enjoying being a teenager.

"I most certainly will not!" — replied Tiso, angrily, because he knew that he himself was probably going to Hell, no matter how often he processed to Lauffen.

"You must come to Heaven with me then!" — shouted Jäger, yanking back his hoodie. He grabbed the shocked, fat cleric, swung him up into the air, and whirled him around so wildly that all Tiso's finery fell off, until he was left only in his red silk underpants and white socks, spinning through the blue sky.

"There you go, Fatty! That's what Heaven looks like." — yelled Mr. Jäger. On the ground, the two, blond — no longer strong — collection plate boys, fell on their knees, and wept. Someone in the congregation, shrieked. An old lady fainted.

Mr. Jäger knew, Monsignor Tiso was unkillable... as evil so often is. He dumped Tiso on the Dachstein glacier, and hammered horseshoes onto his knees, chuckling as he worked... "You call yourself a Christian, *Monsignor* — so, you love praying on your knees. Let me help you pray your way home to Ischl."

Monsignor Tiso writhed and wailed, but was soon nailed into a kneeling position. Leaving Tiso groaning, Jäger shot off into the sky, cackling to himself.

Tiso did get home eventually — after laboriously shuffling back on his newly shod, tearing and bloody, knees. He had to have an operation to remove the embedded steel nails and scab-crusted horseshoes. His congregation *knew,* Tiso's escape from *Satan* was a miracle, wrote letters, and nominated Monsignor Tiso to be beatified.

THE HALLSTATT SERPENTS

Hallstatt, Austria, is a world-famous tourist reserve. Forget its Neolithic saltmines, ancient graveyards, proto-Celtic settlement, and, the fairy-tale Alpine village, built up the mountainside so each threshold stands nearly on the roof of the heartbreakingly rustic house below. Forget the waterfall and sparkling stream, in which locals once washed their single set of clothes, before the hawkers of cheap tee-shirts, made the laundering of anything but money obsolete.

Forget the dizzying mountains propping up the sky, and forget the deep, impressive lake. Forget even, the skywalk.

All these pale into insignificance, next to the beautiful — understandably selfie-crazed — tourists. If you wish to enjoy the once-in-a-lifetime spectacle of pullulating, migratory herds of majestic sightseers, come to Hallstatt.

Except... occasionally, in Winter, when Hallstatt is cold, shadowy, and desolate, because the low Sun is blocked out by the mountains. At such a time, older tales come alive.

You alight at the railway stop, on the opposite side of the lake, then take a ferry across the, gently lapping, *Hallstättersee*. If you are lucky, it may be snowing as you chug in to the wood boat-houses and landing stage. There will be no tourists about, as these are more delicate than snowmen, and avoid snow that cannot be skied on.

When you land, walk through the slanted, snow-muted, market square, past its balconied, pastel coloured, Alpine houses. Then, pick your way up the mountainside, on a steep, sometimes stepped, path, traversing the little bridge across the gushing stream that is heard everywhere.

Eventually, you will end up at the top of the village, in the tiny graveyard of the church of *St. Mary on the Mountain.* The Virgin Mary is perfectly capable of travelling through several places simultaneously, and, whether she is *in the shade*, or, *on the mountain*— or even, in a cliff's keyhole with her baby — depends only on her mood. The blessed Virgin is always going everywhere at once, which is why another local church is called, *St Mary by the Road.*

In Hallstatt in Summer, the blessed Virgin uses her binoculars to study the stampeding, wild tourists. In Winter, she gossips with St. Michael, who is in charge of the bone house next door, while he polishes its painted human skulls.

Two of these skulls, are decorated with hook-tailed snakes, which seem to be slithering through the eye-sockets. The hundreds of other brain-wrappers, are painted more conventionally, and are inscribed with the dates of existence and names of their former owners.

These, more conventional, skulls, have one of four different designs: roses (for *love*, on caring, feminine skulls), oak leaves (for *glory*, on self-important, masculine skulls), ivy (for *life,* which no longer clings to the skull), and bay leaves (for *victory*, in some forgotten punch-up). Terror of anonymity, pervades the dead of Hallstatt, which is why it has the largest collection of painted skulls on Earth.

Hallstatt has always been a busy place, and the graveyard is as overcrowded with guests as the village. So, the dead have pioneered an innovative hotel concept: after a fifteen-year staycation in the earth, they are dug up and washed, then bleached by the Sun and Moon for a few weeks. The skeletons are politely disassembled and stacked. The skulls are painted and lovingly displayed above the bones. Graveyard hotel-rooms are freed up for new visitors.

The horror of being forgotten — of a life completely uncared about — must be overwhelming in Hallstatt, to have produced such a tradition.

There is good reason for this.

Before Hallstatt existed, a town called *Cervusau*, stood underneath where the lake now shimmers, at the foot of the Zwoelferkogel and Rauchkogel mountains, in a shadowy corner of the Hirschau. The mighty fort, *Stutato,* towered above it on Salt Mountain, near the entrance to the famous Neolithic saltmines. Cervusau's inhabitants were smugly content because they lived in such a lovely area: nothing undermined their existence... except, the undermining monsters gnawing away in the earth.

The Cervusauers, arrogantly dismissed, reports of *Tearers of Corpses:* giant, tunneling serpents, longer than a road tunnel, which still occasionally collapse mineshafts with their insatiable binge-eating.

One lovely morning, Cervusau basked in the Sun. By the afternoon, it was underwater and all its people drowned.

Such is life.

The *Tearers of Corpses* had come home to feast and give birth, as they do every five centuries. These titanic serpents behave similarly to adders, which slither across Austria to reproduce, back to the mountains that spawned them. Because they are adapted to a cool climate, baby serpents seem to be born, not hatched from eggs. The mother-snake carries the fertilised eggs and warms them in her own body, until her brood is ready to hatch.

Generating enough heat for hatching *Tearers of Corpses,* needs more energy than gobbling up the plants, people, and animals, of the Salzkammergut, could ever provide — so, rocks, underground salt, and earth, are all ferociously devoured by the mothers.

After an orgy of feasting and tunneling, a mighty, crashing, flashflood, filled in the serpent-hollowed cauldron between the mountains, destroying the proud town of Cervusau, and creating the *Hallstättersee.*

Millions of gallons of water, rushed down from the mountain tops, causing mudslides — burying Stutato forever — as giant serpents frolicked in the new lake.

The serpents departed, the waters settled, and a wilderness grew up. Some wanderers discovered the abandoned saltmines, sniffed a commercial opportunity, and built Hallstatt. Cervusauers died, unknown, uncared about, and unmourned, leaving behind only the terror of anonymous death as their legacy... so, why are there two nameless skulls in St. Michael's chapel, painted with images of hooktailed serpents?

Hallstatt once had a witch — it may have had more than one, but this witch was called Vroni, and it was long before she met her future husband, Hans Wurst. Young Vroni was simply known as *die Hexe,* as beautiful young women so often are.

Vroni was unpopular with other Hallstatt girls, because she was a startlingly self-assured orphan, as well as, redhaired and beautiful. Her eyes were emerald, like those of the damned. She was poisonously rumoured to cast spells on young men, to make them fall in love with her.

Through no fault of her own, Vroni became fashionable. It was obvious that every young man in Hallstatt was mad keen to be with Vroni — and this, alas, was impossible.

When the young men realised they could not all partner Vroni, they gave up, and became hostile. It was easier to go along with whatever their recent, less glamorous, girlfriends, hissed at them, every time Vroni passed on the street.

"Look at that witch! Walking around like she owns the place." — a girl might hiss, to her own, sheepishly nodding, boyfriend. This was always said loudly so Vroni would hear. At first, she ran after her haters, and argued... "Please, I'm not a witch. I hardly own anything."

Couples would stop, glare at Vroni like she was a disease they wished to avoid, then stride off arm in arm.

Vroni did not comprehend, why friendly boys were growing up into angry men. And she never understood why girls hated her. Vroni desperately desired to enter the walled city of everyday pleasantries, of "*Hellos*" and "*How-are-yous?*", but was made to understand: a witch has no place there.

Vroni's self-assurance shrivelled. Her life consisted of tramping through the forest to gather windfall nuts and fruit for herself, and hard-to-get, medicinal herbs — to sell from her home, to frowning, snarling, underpaying customers.

Her only friends were a stray, skin-and-bones, piebald cat, she took in and named *Kitten,* and an old, black cockerel, called *Rooster*, which she bought to save from the cooking pot. These pets added to her reputation for being a witch.

Each night, Vroni got down on her knees and prayed to be accepted by her neighbours, pleading with any higher power that would listen — because God never answered her prayers.

One sunny lunchtime, two feared locals, universally called *the Snake Men,* knocked on Vroni's door. They were the snake men because of the story of serpents having hooked tails to grab onto the earth, to resist God's wish to pluck them up into Heaven. Men like these were (supposedly) so attached to earthly things, their souls slithered on the ground — or through the gutter, if one was available.

The men were rumoured, known, reputed sodomites. Nobody respectable invited them indoors. They both had emerald eyes, just like Vroni, and each wore a black mask, with a black, broad-brimmed hat, and a black cloak.

"Please, come in!" — said Vroni, delighted to have visitors — "Can I get you something... perhaps, some Ironweed tea?"

"Thank you, Fräulein — you are too kind. Tea, please." — said the first man, entering Vroni's hovel. His companion followed, and they both sat down at the wonky table, which had seen better days — as had the chairs they sat on. As had all Vroni's hovel.

Vroni boiled up some Ironweed leaves in a copper kettle on the hearth, then carefully strained the tea into cracked, china cups, and, smiling, handed them to her guests. These, took off their hats and masks, revealing young, gleamingly unlined, faces. Both men were completely bald, without eyebrows, or beards. They were so pink and smooth, Vroni could not help but stare at them in wonder.

"Marmot." — said the first man, looking at his companion, who suppressed a smirk as he loudly slurped tea — "The secret of our great complexions is rendered marmot fat."

"I'm sorry, sir. I don't understand." — said Vroni.

The second man explained... "The best moisturiser for your face is made from boiled marmots — also called, *gophers.* We sell our moisturiser in the market. I'm surprised you have not noticed us... it is a great hit with the young ladies of Hallstatt."

"The *young ladies* never talk to me." — said Vroni, more bitterly than she intended,

"I'm sorry to hear that. By the way, I'm Flo — Florian — and this is Jo — Johann."

"Delighted to make your acquaintance. Vroni." — said Vroni.

Jo nodded and sipped his tea.

Flo smiled.

Vroni nearly wept with joy. Her prayers had been answered, and she wanted to cherish her two new friends... even if they did boil up gophers. Their friendly, wrinkle-free faces, were worth a few boiled gophers.

"You are a very kind lady, Vroni." — said Flo — "You haven't even asked us why we are visiting you. You just straightaway offered us hospitality."

"You really are most kind." — added Jo.

This was too much. Vroni started to weep.

"Please, don't cry." — said Flo, standing up and offering Vroni a black handkerchief, "We have been aware of your prayers for a while now. The higher power we serve, sent us to find out if you are worthy of a gift granted only to the most special people. I am delighted to say: you are worthy."

Vroni blew her nose. It was the first time Vroni had been offered a gift by anyone.

Jo stood up, reached into his cloak, and pulled out, what looked like parchment. As he unrolled it, Vroni saw it was a contract. He handed it to her to read...

I, Vroni, known as 'the Witch', hereafter known as 'the Stormbride', agree to take over guardianship of all the storms, lightning, and winds, in my area. In return, these will serve me faithfully and do my bidding until their dying breath.

Signed, Vroni, the Stormbride, nee, the Witch

"_____"

Vroni's delight turned to puzzlement.

"I didn't pray for this." — said Vroni, wiping her face on her sleeve — "What, in Heaven's name, would I do with a storm?"

Jo seemed insulted by her reaction. "What we pray for and what we get, are two different things." — he said, huffily — "Here." He thrust a quill and an ink well at Vroni.

Flo tried to soothe Vroni... "You're a bright girl, Vroni — you'll think of something. Storms usually die anonymous and unloved, because nobody wants a storm near them. You're exactly the right person to help storms find companionship, because nobody wants you near them either. Surely, you sympathise with the loneliness of storms?"

"Storms aren't lonely." — retorted Vroni, "They don't have feelings."

"That's what people always say about shunned beings — to comfort themselves after the thing's died." — said Flo... "But, just think, what are storms like while they're alive? Have you ever seen a storm that didn't seem upset?"

When Vroni thought about it: she did sympathise with storms. People always swore at storms like they did at Vroni. People always hid indoors from storms, like they did from Vroni. And, girls always hissed at their boyfriends, if they met a storm coming down the street... just like they did when meeting Vroni.

Yet, Vroni had never heard of such a contract — let alone, any way of enforcing it. Flo and Jo must be teasing her, like friends are supposed to. Vroni was glad she now had friends who teased her. Vroni signed, to show she was a good sport.

"Just one thing, Vroni..." — said Jo, taking back the parchment, his quill, and his ink well — "To make sure you keep to the contract, we'll send you another little present. You will know what it is once it arrives. Don't be frightened of it... so long as you keep to our bargain, it will not harm you."

"Thank you for your hospitality, Vroni. We wish you a lovely day." — said Flo, putting on his mask and hat to leave.

Jo put his on too.

"Please, don't go... wouldn't you like some more Ironweed tea?" — said Vroni, anxious not to lose her new friends.

"I'm sorry, but we need to visit the priest of St. Mary's. He has been rather unkind about us in his sermons." — said Jo, through his mask.

"Yes, we have to go." — added Flo.

"Will I see you again?" — asked Vroni.

"Who knows?" — shrugged Jo, exiting onto the street — "Don't forget now. You've got another present coming."

Flo tipped his hat, and followed his partner out the door.

Teary-eyed — sad, yet elated — Vroni stared at *the Snake Men,* until they disappeared around the corner.

The next morning before dawn, Rooster crowed loudly and flapped his wings. Kitten arched her back, and spat — hissing at Vroni like a Hallstatt girl might. Catapulted out of a panic-stricken dream of being burnt as a witch, Vroni jumped out of bed — though, not as fast as her heart did.

Vroni looked around her shabby bedroom, to reassure herself it was empty. "What's wrong with you?" — she said, stroking the hissing cat, as her cockerel continued to flap, making Vroni cough with the dust from his wings.

Rooster gave one, ringing, cock-a-doodle-doo, laid a huge black egg, froze rigid, and fell over dead. Vroni nearly fainted with the shock. Kitten, scratched Vroni's hand, and dashed off.

Vroni stared at her dead pet — and at the impossible egg that killed him. Perhaps, this egg was Flo and Jo's gift to her? How it might help Vroni keep to her contract was a riddle.

Should Vroni boil the egg and eat it? No. .. the egg was too spooky for eating. Maybe, the egg had nothing to do with Flo and Jo?

Vroni decided to hatch the egg, regardless of who it was from. In the meantime, Vroni would — regretfully — boil up Rooster, and eat him. Vroni gathered some wood, fired up her hearth, and stuck the plucked cockerel in a pot, with water and herbs. She carefully wrapped the egg in rags, and secreted it in her bosom to start incubating it.

Rooster was not a great meal, but he was food. After eating him, Vroni devoted herself to weeks of carrying the egg in her bosom by day, and bedding it down on a pillow at night. She was as tender towards that egg as any attentive mother is to her baby. Vroni felt she owed it to her dead cockerel, even though he did not taste nice.

One morning, after seven weeks — as the first sunbeams touched the egg on its pillow — the shell glowed pink. The egg shook and creaked, until — it cracked and shattered. Some shards hit Vroni in the face.

As Vroni watched, dumb-struck, a baby serpent wriggled out of the broken egg, stretched, and looked around quizzically.

He noticed Vroni looking at him — and straightaway slid up Vroni's skirt, over her corset, and down Vroni's cleavage, coming to rest between her breasts.

Vroni gazed down at her cleavage. The little snake gazed back — and, Vroni could have sworn he grinned.

"I will call you, *Snake.*" — whispered Vroni, because, despite being interesting, she was not very imaginative when naming pets.

It soon became apparent, the concord between mother and stepson would not last. Snake had a voracious appetite, and, no matter what Vroni fed him, it was never enough. Snake stole Kitten's food, disposed of all the mice in the house, and — finally — gobbled up Kitten.

"Bad boy, Snake! Naughty!" — yelled Vroni. She cold-shouldered the serpent for a couple of days, and would not let him snuggle up with her — but then, Snake stared at her so imploringly, soulfully, and unblinkingly, she let him back into her bosom.

Vroni took Snake with her to forage in the forest. When she released the little beast from her corset, he dashed off, tunnelling through the leaves, chomping on windfall apples, snapping at any creature he could find, no matter how large. He nearly caught a fox, then slithered up a tree, and devoured an entire nest of squawking chicks.

Looking pleased with himself, Snake came down again, sluggishly climbed Vroni's leg — and slept in Vroni's bosom all the way home.

Vroni did not like babysitting a serpent gourmand, and wondered why Flo and Jo had inflicted him on her. She still had no idea how to summon, let alone befriend, a storm. In fact, she thought Flo and Jo had played a joke on her — most likely, on behalf of other Hallstätters.

The baby serpent gobbled up all the mice, birds, cats, and dogs, in the neighbourhood. Then, he started on the pigs, goats, and donkeys. Vroni's neighbours, blamed Vroni for the disappearance of their pets and livestock. Yet, there was nothing Vroni could do about it, and she denied all knowledge when the crone next-door complained.

"Fräulein, where's my poodle? Everyone knows, you're a nasty witch who makes things disappear!" — yelled the crone, almost falling over herself with rage.

"I have no idea what's happened to your stupid dog! Maybe, you ate it while you were asleep, you silly old Moo?" — shouted Vroni, confirming every prejudice her neighbour had about her.

Vroni slammed the door, and scolded her serpent — hissing under her breath so her neighbour would not hear. Vroni did not like hissing. Snake was becoming way too influential on her life.

Early one morning, as the Sun reddened the mountains, Vroni got up and prodded Snake, who was dozing by the hearth. She had decided to smuggle Snake down to Hallstatt Lake in a handcart, so he could gorge himself on wild fishes instead of on her neighbours' animals. Snake was heavy. It was hard, stopping the cart from pulling her down the slope.

When they reached the lakeshore, Snake emerged from the old blanket Vroni had hidden him under, looked around, flickered his tongue, and shot off into the lake. Snake did not straightaway start guzzling fishes, but enjoyed himself, frolicking like the ancient *Tearers of Corpses* that created the lake.

Vroni watched Snake, delighted — until he bumped into a little rowing boat.

The fisherman in the boat, heard Vroni yell at Snake, saw her panicked face before he himself hit the water — and instantly knew, everything bad was Vroni's fault.

Vroni worried, Snake might gobble up the fisherman... then, she reflected — if Snake did gobble him up — well, it would be one less annoyance in the world.

(In fact, there was no danger of Snake gobbling up humans. He considered Vroni to be his mother, and would not attack any creature that looked like her.)

After devouring a shoal of *Reinanke* fish, and two, very surprised, swans, Snake dragged himself ashore. He was now too fat to get back in the handcart, so Vroni covered him in his blanket, and encouraged him to slither home up the mountain.

"Go on, you stupid worm!" — ordered Vroni, nervously eyeing the fisherman, who was swimming to shore — "You've caused enough trouble for one day."

She kicked Snake, who stared back at her in puzzled anguish.

"Go on! Move!" — yelled Vroni, pointing towards the church of St. Mary's at the top of Hallstatt.

Comprehending what his mother wanted him to do, Snake, shrugged, as only an overfed serpent can — and started to haul himself uphill.

Vroni began laboriously to push the handcart after Snake — halting every now and then to pick up his blanket when it slipped off, to cover him again.

The blanket fooled none of the Hallstätters, who peered through their shutters at Vroni and Snake. They knew, without knowing or being told: Vroni was a witch and Snake was Lucifer.

Gossip deluged Hallstatt, like one of the village's occasional mudslides.

At home, Snake gobbled — and gulped — and guzzled — and grew and grew, until he was longer than a small tunnel and wider than a roadside ditch. He no longer fitted inside Vroni's hovel, even when coiled, and had to sleep with his tail hanging out of the window.

One morning, the crone nextdoor, caught Snake, furtively devouring a pig she had bought to fatten for Winter. As Snake swallowed the sow, the animal fought back and squealed, never realising, she had escaped being turned into pork fillets, ribs, ham, sausages, puddings, and bacon. Being eaten by a serpent was no consolation. Her owner too, was not a person who indulged exotic fauna — especially not, when said fauna belonged to a witch, and was devouring her pig.

The crone was old enough not to be scared of anything. She fetched her broom and repeatedly whacked Snake.

"Stop it, you nasty thing! STOP IT! You wait, until I get hold of your mistress." — she yelled, hitting Snake with all her might.

It is impossible to say if Snake noticed.

The serpent left the crone's house with a big, wriggling bulge in his belly. He slithered back in, through the window of Vroni's hovel, but could not get his expanded waistline through the gap, so he went to sleep with even more of his tail hanging out than usual.

The crone did not bother knocking on Vroni's door to complain. She knocked on every other door she knew. Sanctimonious rage made the old lady feel young. Her fellow burghers too, were infantilised by their hatred, and became a seething crowd of children out for Vroni's blood.

"Burn the witch!" — whispered the new children to each other, chuckling as they lit their torches.

They were *hangry*. None of them had eaten anything substantial since Snake arrived in their neighbourhood: Snake had gobbled up every tasty beast.

Vroni was dozing by her hearth, wondering what she was going to do that day. She had breakfasted on nettle soup and roast beetroot, and gone back to sleep. Snake was still sleeping off the pig, which had finally stopped kicking inside his belly. The first sign of danger was the smell of burning wood.

Vroni did not stir.

The lynch mob kept quiet, to make sure they burnt themselves a witch, instead of merely spooking her.

 Numbed by smoke, Vroni dreamt someone was lighting a delicious barbecue. Snake had the inborn fear of fire of all animals, and uncoiled himself to peek outside, where his tail was already twitching. He knocked over the pot of nettle soup with a loud clatter, waking Vroni.

"God, Snake! Can't you watch out?" — chided Vroni, not realising that Snake was watching out.

Then, Vroni opened one sleepy eye and saw the room was full of smoke. She opened her other eye, and saw flames devouring the walls of her hovel. A cheer erupted outside, as a blazing wooden beam tumbled from her roof.

Instantly, Vroni was wide awake.

Snake, turned, flicked his tail at the mob, and tunnelled deep into the ground.

"Back to Hell, where you came from!" — said a Hallstatt girl, winking at her boyfriend — never realising that *Hell* is located under Lauffen village.

Terrified, Vroni panicked. Before she knew what she was doing, Vroni started to whistle her favourite waltz. Black storm clouds thickened above her hovel. Lightning crackled and thunder banged, while some insane, invisible, orchestra, imperturbably and relentlessly, played the Blue Danube waltz by Johann Strauss Jr.

A whirlwind lifted Vroni through the smoke, up, up into the sky, high above her burning home.

The mob was no longer bent on murder, but infected with fear. Rain swept down the mountain, extinguishing the fire, drenching the screaming, fleeing Hallstätters, as they tripped over each other, trying to get away from no danger at all.

Vroni spun through the thunderstorm, faster and faster, until she was too dizzy to see where she was. Her tongue was wedged into the side of her mouth by the g-forces. The air became too thin to breathe. Finally, the whirlwind gently set Vroni down in the Zimnitz valley.

Snake was never seen again. Nor were any other *Tearers of Corpses*. It is said, the two, anonymous skulls painted with snakes, and displayed in the bone house, protect Hallstatt against the return of the giant serpents.

Flo and Jo had visited the thoughtlessly sermonising priest, who turned out also to be a rumoured, known, reputed sodomite, as so many priests are. He was friendlier than they expected.

When the priest died many years later, he left provision in his will, for Flo and Jo's skulls to be painted with snakes and placed near his own skull — to show they were loved.

THE DRAGON

In a cave, in the high cliffs above Moon Lake called *Dragon Cliffs,* lived a dragon named, *Friedensreich.* He was not some leftover from Prehistory. He had been conceived as a human child, but rejected. Cursed by his mother at his ugly birth, he had grown up into a fully-fledged, fire-breathing lizard with wings.

Friedensreich's body — the scaly, reptilian body of his own, cursed being — is not so different in character to the beautiful bodies of the blessed. Both cursed and blessed bodies, are treated as entertaining spectacles by those with commonplace bodies... which is why, dragons are usually depicted with a blessed, beautiful maiden.

Dragons hanker after beautiful maidens — but, alas, beautiful maidens do not often hanker after dragons. Even when beautiful maidens age, and turn into dragons themselves, they still do not hanker after dragons. They are glad to see dragons slain, because the dragon is a symbol of their own aged selves, which they prefer to ignore.

Friedensreich's prospects of finding a mate were not good, because he never met anybody. He only flew at night, so as to avoid ignorant people, who threw stones and bottles at him. He avoided the early morning and its hunters' rifles.

Friedensreich sailed above the mountains, forests, and lakes, looked down at the towns shining in the valleys, and felt lonely. It is hard to find that one, special girl, when you are a two-legged lizard with bat's wings.

One balmy night, a warm, steady breeze was blowing, which meant Friedensreich could fly further than usual. (He had to glide everywhere, so as not to attract attention with his flapping wings.) A full Moon lit up the night. Those who saw Friedensreich block out the stars, merely thought he was a newfangled hang-glider.

Friedensreich let himself drift all the way from Moon Lake, to a mountain he had never seen before. He circled above it to take a closer look.

Between the trees, he noticed a splashy, little stream by a *Forststrasse.* The stream, was strewn with boulders, and hidden, but Friedensreich could hear the water, and Friedensreich realised he felt thirsty. It was similar to the feeling Friedensreich got when he heard girls' voices.

Friedensreich raised his wings for the descent, flapped a couple of times to ease his landing, and silently touched down on the *Mountain Of Women,* though he did not know this was its name. Friedensreich looked around nervously, to check he was alone... and saw, a very voluptuous, naked woman, staring at him in amazement.

Friedensreich ducked behind an oak. He peeked tentatively round the tree trunk, hoping he was more inconspicuous than dragons usually are, and found himself face to face with an enormous breast.

Startled, Friedensreich staggered back, tripped over a root, and landed heavily on his back, crumpling his wings. The breast too, seemed startled, and lurched backwards — which enabled Friedensreich to see that the breast had a twin, and belonged to the voluptuous woman. She had crept up on him.

Now, she towered over him.

"Hello, darling!" — said the voluptuous woman — "And who might you be then?"

"Er, er, Friedensreich." — stammered Friedensreich, feeling very awkward as he struggled up... "B-but, my friends, if I had any, would p-probably call me Freddie."

"Eva." — said Eva, holding out her hand to shake one of Freddie's talons.

Freddie shyly took her hand, and kissed it: a romantic gesture he had often read about, but never before attempted. It did not occur to Freddie to ask why Eva was naked. As a dragon, naturism was second nature to him. It was clothes that he found odd. Freddie thought Eva looked lovely. Yet, Eva had let herself go in the last year.

When her life with Mr. Jäger proved miserable, Eva sought solace in cream cakes and beer. At first, Mr. Jäger had forced her to diet, but then he met an unlucky new girl — and now, he mostly ignored Eva, for which she thanked Heaven.

Eva had gotten fatter and fatter, until her body looked perpetually about to explode. Yet, because Eva was young and her face remained beautiful, she was still expected to entice souls into Mr. Jäger's clutches. Otherwise, he cut off her cream cakes and beer.

Surprised and flattered by Freddie's gallant greeting, Eva smiled, despite her depression, and said... "Well, that's introductions out of the way. Now, I know who you are. But *what* are you?"

Freddie was embarrassed by this question.

He liked to pretend dragons were fantasies. Freddie never liked to admit that he himself was a dragon — especially not, in front of a pretty girl like Eva. Yet, Freddie's wings and scaly skin tended to give him away.

"I'm a - a - a man." — stammered Freddie.

"You're not! You look like a dragon, not that I've seen one before."

"Well, I sup-pose that's one way of looking at it. But, but, I'm a man. Mostly."

"Do you take your wings and scales off before bed?"

"N-no."

"Well, if you look like a dragon, and you fly like a dragon, then you must be a dragon! I wouldn't worry about it, darling... but, I must get on."

A light went on in the Hellhole, meaning, Mr. Jäger was on his way. Eva hissed at Freddie... "Just get away from me. Hide!"

This was more like the usual reaction of beautiful maidens to Freddie. He scrambled for cover, tripped over, and landed on his wings again. A furious, drunken Mr. Jäger, loomed up behind Eva. The engorged vein on his forehead pulsed like a maggot.

"Who the fuck is this?" — slurred Mr. Jäger.

"Nobody, darling. It's just a dragon. Nothing to interest you." — said Eva, soothingly.

"I'll be the fucking judge of that!" — yelled Mr. Jäger.

"My na-name's Freddie." — stammered Freddie, unsuccessfully trying to get up.

"Who asked you, croc-head?" — shouted Mr. Jäger.

Mr. Jäger, turned his blazing eyes on Eva, and screamed... "What have I told you about wasting my time? Where's my fucking souls?"

"I'm, I, I mean — I'm sorry. I got distracted. I'll get you one before tomorrow, I promise." — stammered Eva, mirroring Freddie's anxiety.

"One? You fucking lazy, fat, good-for-nothing whore!" — screamed Mr. Jäger, and backhanded Eva so hard one of her teeth loosened.

She crashed down onto Freddie.

"I think you'd better leave." — whispered Eva, to Freddie, blood welling from her top lip.

"Yeah, piss off!" — snorted Mr. Jäger, and kicked Eva.

Freddie knew, Jäger was evil.

"Get away from her!" — shouted Freddie, baring his fangs. He put a protective talon in front of Eva.

"Oh yeah?" — screamed Mr. Jäger, and kicked Freddie in the stomach.

Freddie was unable to stand up for Eva.

Writhing in pain, Freddie shielded Eva's eyes with his wing and roared. A needle-sharp blast of fire erupted from the depths of Freddie's sweet, outraged soul, instantly scorching Jäger's genitals. Mr. Jäger howled and danced, trying to flee the agony.

He could not.

Mr. Jäger's penis was a smouldering wick. His testicles were two, tiny, charcoal briquettes.

Freddie seized Eva in his talons and took off. He had never carried anyone before — and Eva was hefty. Freddie could not glide, but was forced to rapidly flap his wings to stay airborne.

As they ascended from the Mountain Of Women, Eva heard Mr. Jäger's mummified, immortal exes giggling: two words, repeating over and over, echoing on the rocks, gurgling in the stream, whispering through the trees:.. *"No balls, no balls, no balls, no..."*

Eva and Freddie were sky-high.

Freddie panted more and more heavily, as he lugged Eva towards Moon Lake. Eva was silent. Her escape from Mr. Jäger had not yet sunk in.

When they got close to Freddie's cave, the effort of hauling Eva's voluptuous body became too much for Freddie. He crashed into the side of the rock face, denting it so hard with Eva's buttocks that, the hollow he made, is still known as *Dragon's Dent.*

Freddie had to make an emergency landing.

Eva touched down, bruised and dazed. Freddie was apologetic... "I'm so, so sorry! I d-didn't mean t-to b-bang you into the mountain. Are you a-alright?"

"I've had worse." — said Eva, and fainted.

Freddie gently carried Eva back to his cave. He made a sweet-scented bed of leaves and flowers, laid Eva down on it, and watched over her.

When Eva woke up two days later, the first thing she asked was for Freddie to take her to Adama. Freddie took a deep breath, braced himself, lifted Eva up in his talons, and dragged her through the air to Kreutern.

Adama was delighted to see her sister. She also liked Freddie. So, the three of them moved in together and were happy. And their lives accelerated, as happy lives do. Eva fell in love with Freddie — and Eva lost weight — not, because she dieted — but because she was happy — and she swilled less beer — and she gobbled fewer cream cakes — and Freddie lost his virginity to Eva — and Freddie blossomed — and Freddie adored Eva — and Eva adored Freddie — and Abel came home — (the old man of the Zimnitz could not cope once Abel hit puberty) — and Abel settled in nicely — and, the old man of the Zimnitz gave them gold (to say sorry) — and Adama stayed happy — and Eva stayed happy — and Freddie stayed happy — and Abel stayed happy. And... they all lived happily ever after.

Mr. Jäger stayed an impotent laughing stock, even after he had a prosthetic penis fitted.

As they ascended from the Mountain Of Women, Eva heard, Mr. Jäger's mummified, immortal exes giggling: two words, repeating over and over, echoing on the rocks, gurgling in the stream, whispering through the trees:.. *"No balls, no balls, no balls, no... "*

Eva and Freddie were sky-high.

Freddie, panted more and more heavily, as he lugged Eva towards Moon Lake. Eva was silent. Her escape from Mr. Jäger had not yet sunk in.

When they got close to Freddie's cave, the effort of hauling Eva's voluptuous body became too much for Freddie. He crashed into the side of the rock face, denting it so hard with Eva's buttocks, that, the hollow he made, is still known as *Dragon's Dent.*

Freddie had to make an emergency landing.

Eva touched down, bruised and dazed. Freddie was apologetic... "I'm so, so sorry! I d-didn't mean t-to b-bang you into the mountain. Are you a-alright?"

"I've had worse." — said, Eva, and fainted.

Freddie, gently carried Eva back to his cave. He made a sweet-scented bed of leaves and flowers, laid Eva down on it, and watched over her.

When Eva woke up two days later, the first thing she asked was for Freddie to take her to Adama. Freddie, took a deep breath, braced himself, lifted Eva up in his talons, and dragged her through the air to Kreutern.

Adama was delighted to see her sister. She also liked Freddie. So, the three of them moved in together, and were happy. And their lives accelerated, as happy lives do. Eva fell in love with Freddie — and Eva lost weight — not, because she dieted — but because she was happy — and she swilled less beer — and she gobbled fewer cream cakes — and Freddie lost his virginity to Eva — and Freddie blossomed — and Freddie adored Eva — and Eva adored Freddie — and Abel came home — (the old man of the Zimnitz could not cope once Abel hit puberty) — and Abel settled in nicely — and, the old man of the Zimnitz gave them gold (to say sorry) — and Adama stayed happy — and Eva stayed happy — and Freddie stayed happy — and Abel stayed happy. And... they all lived happily ever after.

Mr. Jäger stayed an impotent laughing stock, even after he had a prosthetic penis fitted.

Moon Lake

A long time ago, some fishermen drowned on Moon Lake, in the shadow of Dragon Cliffs. Their bodies were lost. A crucifix was put on a rock in the lake to remember them, and a vine grew around it.

The bodies of the fishermen dissolved into the lake, and their skeletons got picked clean by fishes — who were unaware of the irony — and the fishermen's bones broke up and sank down, and were lost in the warm mud of the lake.

The fishermen's loved ones, cried for a bit, cheered up, and later on — died.

Those fishermen became part of the water and of the fishes. People swam in them, people ate them, and people watered their gardens with them. Sometimes, people read about them.

The Sun shone down on Moon Lake. The Moon shone down on Moon Lake. It rained and it snowed.

The fishermen fermented into a myth.

RAUHNACHT

Suddenly, I was a little boy — in bed in the old kitchen I used to sleep in as a child, watching paper snakes, which Oma had made to help me sleep. I watched them twist on the wood-stove, as they made grotesque shadows on the white-washed wall, glimmering in the reflected flames from the stove.

It was Winter and, once the fire burnt out, the condensation on the window panes would sprout ice-daisies. I pulled up my covers, and wriggled down into the warmth, imagining myself as a happy serpent in a hollow.

I enjoyed the snakes spinning on their bases. Oma made them from discs of paper, cut inward towards the centre in a spiral — the centre was a snake's head, the tail tapered towards the end. She balanced the heads on pins stuck in splints of firewood, wedged into cotton reels.

The hot air from the stove made them spin.

A log cracked.

I remembered fireworks and gunshots, used to drive out angry spirits on a *Rauhnacht*. I have never understood, why ghosts should be scared of explosions and bullets. Perhaps, it is the drunken jollity of the gunmen, which puts them off. Maybe, the dead are no party animals?

Some dead people also get rather anxious — but the dead who come out on Rauhnächte, do not suffer from anxiety. They are not even scared of the frankincense, melting, sizzling, and smoking on stove tops to purify the air of evil.

Rauhnächte are nights when the Wild Hunt gallops across the sky, searching for souls to steal. If you are caught outdoors, the hunters will drag you away with them. If you peep at them through a keyhole, it makes the hunters so self-conscious they blind you with one of their arrows. The damned do not like being stared at.

I do not know how long I lay there, pondering ghosts galloping across an Alpine Heaven. I must have fallen asleep. I woke up because I was thirsty and needed to go downstairs for a drink of water.

The fire was burnt out and the snakes had stopped turning. The kitchen froze. My throat felt dry and lined with tiny, sharp, icicles, which pricked me every time I opened my mouth to breathe.

I tore back the bedcovers — exposing my warm body to the night, with an instant, shocking rush of cold. I had to tread carefully, so as not to disturb my grandparents, who slept in the bedroom opposite me.

The air bristled as I crept towards the landing.

I fretted in the dark, when there was nothing — like my eiderdown — to hold on to. Growing up in forests and mountains, has given me a distrust of gloomy, open spaces.

It was a relief to bang my hip on a table's corner... something solid in the darkness. I felt my way along the table edge. I found the door to the landing, twisted its handle, and opened it.

The skylight above the landing, framed the full Moon, stars, and luminous white clouds. I could see where I was going. I rubbed my bruised hip.

The downstairs light was on.

Voices drifted up the stairs.

One voice sounded like it belonged to my great-aunt, Emmi — a large, red-faced, blonde, who often gave me traffic-light-coloured, boiled sweets, and herbal limonade. She was talking to Oma.

I peeked around the corner of the wooden staircase. My great-aunt had her back to me. The tiny icicles in my throat made me cough.

My great-aunt turned to face me, and smiled.

I realised she was dead.

Terrified, I scrambled back up the stairs. The door on the landing no longer had a handle. I shoved and punched it.

The door stayed shut.

My heart thumped and thumped and thumped. My heartbeat became too strong for my chest.

I woke in a sweat — and saw I was an adult in a bright morning, not a little boy in the dark. My bed was large and new, and I had my own bedroom. Outside my window, leaves sparkled green in the breeze, and on the road, a car sounded its horn. I had central heating now.

I was in a city — many years and miles from the rural superstitions of my childhood. The sweat on my body began to dry. I got up and made a leisurely search for clothes in my wardrobe. I dressed and went to breakfast in the kitchen.

Savouring my vitamin-injected breakfast cereal, I contrasted it with the black bread, butter, and ham, I breakfasted on as a child. Outside, the day shone invitingly. More cars rumbled by.

My mobile rang.

It was my mother — telling me, my great-aunt Emmi had died.

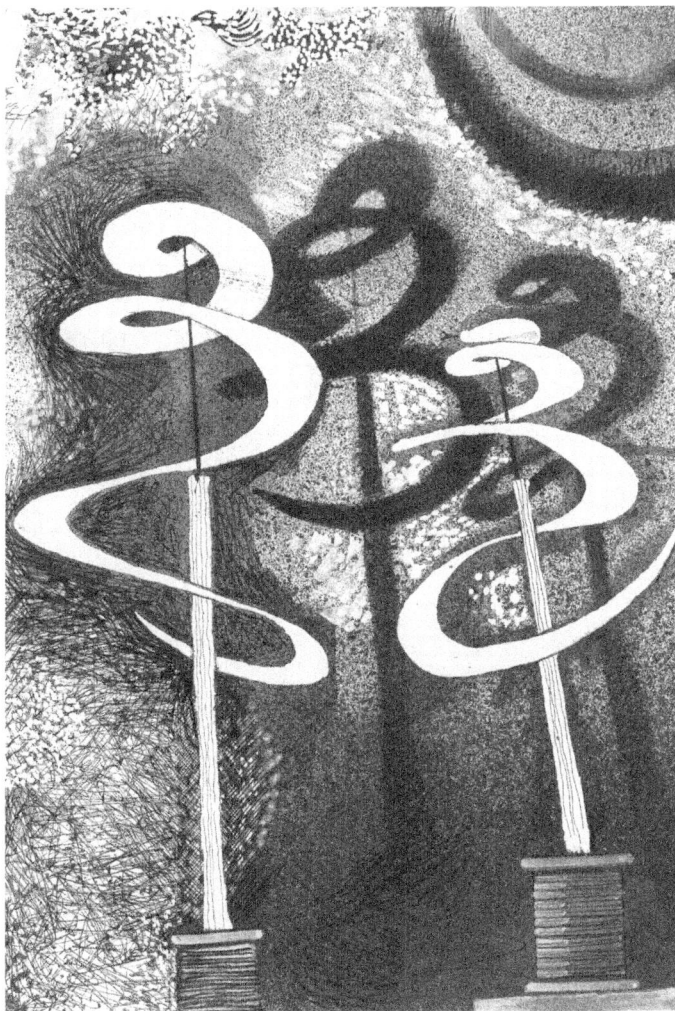

CREDITS

Sunday Pattison, is a writer who lives all over the place, but mostly under your bed.

Jim Anderson, is an English printmaker, painter, and mosaic-maker. He exhibits his artwork internationally; and his public mosaic murals can be found in unexpected places around the world. He lives in Cambridgeshire with his wife Fiona and son Oscar and relaxes by playing the theremin.

www.jimpanzee-art.co.uk

Printed in Dunstable, United Kingdom